Kelly Harte has had many short stories broadcast on BBC Radio 4. This is her first novel. She lives in Yorkshire with her Siamese cat.

TAKING POSSESSION

Anna has left her husband. He's a cheating, lying, miserly rat and her friends agree that she's better off without him. But he refuses to stay out of her life. This can't go on; drastic action is called for. People meet with domestic accidents every day; swallowing garden poison, eating infected food. Why would anyone be suspicious? Why then is it so difficult to execute the plan? But as Anna tries to resolve her life, amid the chaos of past betrayal, new passion, family ties and murderous impulses, it's anybody's guess what direction the future will take.

KELLY HARTE

TAKING POSSESSION

Complete and Unabridged

ULVERSCROFT
Leicester

First published in Great Britain in 1998 by
HarperCollins Publishers
London

First Large Print Edition
published 2000
by arrangement with
HarperCollins Publishers Limited
London

British Library CIP Data

Harte, Kelly
    Taking possession.—Large print ed.—
    Ulverscroft large print series: romance
    1. Separated people—England—Yorkshire—Fiction
    2. Attempted murder—England—Yorkshire—Fiction
    3. Large type books
    I. Title
    823.9′14 [F]

    ISBN 0–7089–4317–9

Published by
F. A. Thorpe (Publishing)
Anstey, Leicestershire

Set by Words & Graphics Ltd.
Anstey, Leicestershire
Printed and bound in Great Britain by
T. J. International Ltd., Padstow, Cornwall

This book is printed on acid-free paper

For Jo and Chris

Soap Operas and Mortuaries

I'm not sure that meditation is all that it's cracked up to be. Indeed, as I sit here in my favourite armchair with my eyes tightly closed, I'm pretty certain it isn't. To achieve relaxation, the idea is to empty the mind completely; but instead of nothingness I keep seeing a man's body on a cold mortuary slab and the dead face I am looking at is Michael's. Then it's useless and no matter how many times I repeat my £400 mantra, I cannot transcend.

And it isn't just meditation I'm having problems with. Lately, I find it difficult to concentrate on anything for long; when it's not in the mortuary, my mind just keeps wandering off in all sorts of unconnected directions. It's definitely getting worse, but I think it all started soon after I moved into my lovely new home with roses growing around its sturdy front door. Yellow roses. My favourite.

I've loved yellow roses since I was a child. I lived then with my parents in an ugly prefab in a run down part of what was actually a very smart Midland town. The only beautiful

1

thing in, or outside that insubstantial little house, was a single yellow rose bush at the end of the garden. How it came to be there was never explained or even wondered about.

Between the pebble-dashed bungalow and the beautiful yellow rose bush, was a concrete pathway and row after row of potato plants. My father was from the Irish countryside and had taken stories about the Great Famine rather too much to heart. Apparently in constant anxiety that the blight would one day return, he alternated the potato varieties he planted annually. 'That was their big mistake,' he told my mother many times, 'not varying the strain.' He had little conversation beyond potato varieties.

Since my father had no time for flowers, regarding all forms of flora as the sentimental whim of soft-hearted females, it is a mystery why I was allowed to keep the rose bush.

I would like to think that I tended that rose bush as if it was my own delicate, possibly consumptive, child, but I didn't. I knew nothing about gardening and, as the years went by in our ugly prefab, it suffered badly from sustained neglect. It fell prey to green fly, black spot and every other form of disease and pestilence from which roses can suffer. But no matter how sickly it became, it always managed to produce a few wonderful blooms.

The roses around my door are perfectly healthy but not nearly so beautiful as the roses of my childhood garden. The blooms are smaller and less vivid in colour. A different variety, I expect, but since I know no more about gardening now than I did when I was a child, I cannot be certain about this. Perhaps the blooms just seem smaller and less vivid than they did to me then.

The interior of my new home is no less attractive than the exterior. It is an estate agent's delight, with beams galore, a pleasantly creaky oak staircase, and a folksy, farmhouse kitchen (which is a bit on the twee side, really, but cosy and comfortable, nevertheless). There is even an ingle-nook fire-place in the sitting room which I can walk into without ducking my head, and I am not a small woman.

It was, however, the rose rather than the charm of the house which sold it to me. I took it as a sign, and my mind was made up to buy the place even before I stepped over the threshold. I've always been susceptible to signs and omens. I know this isn't really a very mature or intelligent way to conduct my life, but then I've made worse decisions than buying this house based on far sounder reasoning.

However, there is a big problem with

abandoning logic completely. It can lead to other superstitious notions, such as my fear that the rose will die in my care because of my ignorance, and that if it does die, my life will go badly wrong. Perhaps I should buy a book about roses and learn how to look after it properly. A little effort would be a small price to pay when so much depends on the rose's survival.

Except if I did buy a book, I don't expect I would read it. I bought one last week about middle-aged women returning to work. I read the first page then shelved it. I just couldn't concentrate on the words, and as for the up-beat, inspirational style it was written in, well, that just depressed me. Besides, I'm not ready to think about earning a living just yet. If I'm honest, the idea frightens me, and I could kill Michael for putting me in this position.

Some people might say I put myself in this position. It was *me*, after all, who left. But I didn't have very much choice in the matter, not once I found out about his affair.

He didn't believe I would go through with it at first. He thought I'd be scared, that given a week or two on my own, I would rush back to him and beg *his* forgiveness. Well, I was scared, but there was no question of going back. Not if I was to keep what remained of my self-respect; I didn't have a lot else and if I'd relinquished that, I might just as well have given up.

So he tried a different tack. He said that I couldn't possibly have loved him if I was prepared to end the marriage because of something so trivial, and that had me going for a while, I admit. It made me feel like the villain of the piece. But then I realised that's exactly what he wanted me to feel, and that it wasn't losing me he was worried about, but a major share of his assets. That was the final straw, the clincher, the *coup de grâce*, the thing which really opened my eyes to what a fool I'd been for so long, and what a bastard Michael really was.

Then he got nasty. He spent a considerable portion of his precious assets ensuring I got as little of what remained as possible; and within a month of my leaving home, he had installed someone else. Not any old someone, but the twenty-two-year-old typist he'd been having the *trivial* affair with. Apart from her age, name and occupation, the only other thing I know about her is that she is a great fan of Oasis. I know this because every time I have had occasion to ring my old home their music has been blaring out in the background, mocking me, advising me not to *look back in anger*.

I accepted far less from Michael than I was entitled to.

My solicitor despaired, pleaded with me to put up a fight — but I wanted things over and done with quickly. And there was enough to buy my home, and a bit left over in the building society, so I'm not complaining. The funny thing is that it's Michael who does all the complaining. He finds it hard to accept that I was entitled to anything, and often rings me to complain about the unfairness of the legal system. And I, because I am a good listener, listen to him, and give in when he asks me for things that were awarded to me by the court. I have no idea why I do this. It makes me resentful. I was very resentful when he took my grandfather clock away. I loved that clock. I loved its dignity, its reliability, and its pretty, reassuring chime. I must have been mad to let it go. Maybe I am a bit mad. I'm certainly not myself — although I'm not even sure what that is any more.

The odd thing is that I must appear all right on the outside. People tell me how well I look, how well I am doing. And I think I was doing well for a while. Until I moved into my new home, that is, and Michael began asking me for my things. It was then that I started seeing him on the mortuary slab.

I get up and flap my arms around a bit, in

the hope it will work off some of this restless energy. But then I catch sight of myself in the mirror by the door and realise that I look as mad as I feel. I am not at all encouraged by this confirmation of my fears so I look round the room for another diversion.

My eyes come to rest on a photograph of my mother and father. Black and white, it is framed in silver and stands amidst similarly framed photos of my daughter Megan on a circular table next to my lumpy, button-backed armchair. There are far more comfortable chairs in the room, but I think of this chair as *my* chair. I sit in it to think my chaotic thoughts and to watch soap operas. I watch them all, avidly. They are the only thing I *can* concentrate on. I am waiting for 'EastEnders' to start now. The TV is on but the sound is turned down on some annoying wildlife programme about seals.

I pick up the photo of my parents which shows them, smiling, on their wedding day. Theirs was a war-time ceremony and apart from the bouquet my mother is holding, there is an absence of frills. She is wearing a pale coloured costume, belted at the waist, which could very nearly pass for elegant. I realise, now, that my mother was once a very pretty woman. Small and delicately framed, with neat, photogenic features. Beside her, my father seems coarse.

I do not resemble either of them. I do not resemble either of them because there is no reason why I should. I was adopted. And like most people who are adopted, I used to fantasise wildly about my real parents. I could never quite see either of them in my mind, but I was always certain that they were very special people. This did not tally well with the fact that they had given me up, however, so I decided that, special as they were, some exciting mystery had prevented them from keeping me. It had been hard, of course, giving me up, but how could they keep me under such exciting and mysterious circumstances? Clearly, however, not a day would have gone by when they did not think about me.

I flop in my chair again and gratefully turn up the sound of the TV. 'EastEnders' has just begun. In no time at all I am blissfully distracted, only then, just when it's getting to the good bit, the telephone rings. Irritated, I leave the answerphone to take the call but when I hear Michael's exasperated voice I sigh and pick up the receiver. I lower the sound of the television with my hand control and keep my eyes on the screen as I half listen to him.

Harsh words are being spoken between two

of the leading characters. I know they are mother and son but not their names. I'm hopeless at remembering the names of soap opera characters.

Michael doesn't bother to ask how I am.

'You know that Millet engraving?' he is saying. 'The one I bought when we were in Jersey.'

I do not answer right away. For a moment it looks like the mother is going to hit her grown-up son with the heavy-looking saucepan she's holding. Then she puts it down, lights up a cigarette, and the tension is broken.

I feel dissatisfied by this, vaguely let down.

'When do you want to pick it up?'

I replace the receiver and close my eyes. Michael is back on the mortuary slab, and this time I'm looking down on him and I'm laughing. Laughing fit to burst.

★　★　★

It is Wednesday 7 June, and I have now been in my new home precisely a month, which means I have been on my own for just over seven months. Not very long considering how much has happened: the separation, finding a temporary flat, squabbles between solicitors, the divorce, the settlement, buying my home, moving, fixing everything up.

I make a note of this milestone on my calendar, and try to think cheerful thoughts. If I have come this far in such a short time, think how far I may go in another seven months. I can do anything I want to if I just put my mind to it.

The morning is sunny and I decide to go for a walk, to clear my head. I had a bad night last night, lots of horrible dreams. In one of the dreams the 'EastEnders' mother with the saucepan was putting her cigarette out in Michael's dead eye. I tried to stop her but only because I thought this was the right thing to do. I didn't really want to stop her. Then, in another snatch from the same dream, or maybe it was a different dream altogether, one of the scallies from 'Brookside' was discussing with his long-suffering wife how to get rid of Michael, which is silly because the villain hasn't been in the soap for ages and his wife wouldn't kill anyone, at least I don't think she would. I seemed to be a character in the soap as well, and I made the suggestion that they cut the brake cords of Michael's car, but the villain shrugged this off. 'That's a crap idea,' he said to me in his strong Liverpudlian accent.

Then I was in Jersey, with Michael. We were in a small gallery in St Hellier, and I found myself drawn to an engraving by Millet; a strange wooded scene with naked cherubs pushing and dragging a half naked woman with an enigmatic expression on her face. And although Michael tried to dissuade me, I was determined to have it. When I woke up I realised this part of the dream was actually more of a recollection. That's how it had been: me, determined to have the engraving, Michael reluctant. I'd bought it with my own money in the end, only of course it wasn't my own money at all because all that I had was really Michael's.

I like where I live now. It is a pretty village of stone-built houses and well tended gardens, and a beck running through its centre. It's almost pretty enough to be a tourist attraction, but fortunately for its residents it lacks that little extra focus of interest. Nothing of historical note has ever occurred here, there are no buildings of real architectural merit, and although it is just the sort of place a Southerner might expect one of those quaint Northern series about loveable vets or cute policemen or whacky old men to be set in, no filming of any kind has ever taken place here.

It has a shop-cum-Post Office which sells most things, a village hall, an okay pub where I had a bar-snack the day I moved into my house, and a pretty Norman church I have not yet been into. I had a visit from the vicar soon after I moved into my new house, but he didn't stay long. I told him what I tell Jehovah's Witnesses when they call at my door — that I am a Catholic — which is only half true as I am no longer a practising Catholic — but it usually does the trick, I find. It seems to have the same effect as telling them that I dabble in black magic. That was certainly the impression I got from the vicar, so I do not expect another visit from him.

I call into the shop to buy a newspaper: the *Sun*, because its sensationalised vision of the world is all I can cope with at the moment. I get it mainly to check Michael's horoscope. If it's bad, it can keep me cheerful all day.

The woman behind the counter has a very warm personality and a strong Lancashire accent. She is always making jokes about being in enemy country, the same joke Yorkshire people make when they move over the border into Lancashire. Her name is Helena Chopin, which strikes me as fairly exotic for a Lancashire postmistress living in Yorkshire.

'You settling in okay now, love?' she asks me. She has asked this often and I give her the same reply:

12

'I'm getting there, thanks.'

I think I am a bit of a mystery in the village. A single, middle-aged woman who doesn't go out to work and keeps herself to herself. I have an idea some of them have me down as a none-too successful Madam, or at least it amuses me to think this is so.

This morning I am the only person in the shop, which is unusual and makes me feel slightly uncomfortable, because Helena Chopin's attention is focused entirely on me. I have the feeling she wants to delve, so I avoid eye contact. But she's not that easily put off.

'I expect you'll be getting back to work soon,' she says.

I find my eyes being drawn to hers against my will. 'I don't have a job,' I tell her, and it comes out feebly, like I've been looking for ages and no one will employ me.

She looks sympathetic, and my heart sinks. All my imagined mysterious glamour gone in an instant. Now I am just a sad, middle-aged woman who can't find a job. 'Don't worry love, something will turn up.'

I force a smile, turn to leave.

'Did you see the poster on the front door?'

I shake my head, turn back to her reluctantly.

'There's a dance in the village hall on

Saturday night, a ceilidh. You should come along, get to know a few people. I've got some tickets here if you'd like one.' She reaches under the counter. 'Only three pounds, pie and pea supper included.'

I feel obliged to buy a ticket although I have no intention of going to the ceilidh. She seems pleased though, and I am pleased to have pleased her.

I slip the pink photocopied ticket into my skirt pocket and leave the shop, forgetting my newspaper. I return and make some original and witty remark along the lines of forgetting my head if it wasn't screwed on. Helena Chopin laughs a little too loudly at this — feels sorry for me, I expect. She's still laughing when the bell on the door pings and a young man comes into the shop.

He's wearing scruffy clothes with holes in his jumper, and his hair is covered in what looks like very coarse talcum powder. It occurs to me that he may have come to hold up the Post Office, so I hover a bit, pretend to find a tin of processed peas fascinating, because I am worried about leaving Helena on her own.

Only it seems my worry is needless.

'What have you been up to, Jack?' says Helena, the laughter still in her voice. 'What's all that in your hair?'

'Plaster,' he says with a big grin, which he turns on me, and I get this funny little feeling in the pit of my stomach which must be embarrassment. 'Just had a ceiling fall in on me.'

I look away, head for the door, don't turn round when Helena calls goodbye.

I miss having the dogs. I feel a bit purposeless without them as I walk through the village. It seemed to make sense at the time to leave them in the house they were used to but I don't like the idea of them wagging their tails for the typist who has taken my place, which I know is very selfish of me, but I can't help my feelings.

I pass a young woman with two small children in a double pushchair. They are squabbling over a tube of Smarties and I feel sorry for the mother. She looks harassed. I offer her a smile of sympathetic understanding, and she returns a brief shrug of gratitude. I try and think of something to say. Something pleasant about the children, perhaps. Mothers like that sort of thing, even when their offspring are behaving like brats. But I'm too slow and they're well down the road before something suitable comes into my head.

I watch a family of ducks darting about on the beck for a while, then return to the house.

15

My spirits are low for some reason, despite the fresh air and exercise. In the kitchen, I put the kettle on the Rayburn and because I know it will take ages to boil, I decide to fetch the Millet engraving, which is upstairs. Michael won't be here till late afternoon, after he finishes work, but I might as well have it ready and waiting.

I make blackcurrant tea and sit at my pine kitchen table. I prop the engraving against the wall and wonder about it. About what's going on exactly in the strange scene.

The phone rings and I leap to answer it before the answerphone cuts in. I'm hoping it's Nell, but it's Michael again.

'Remember those knife handles I framed?'

'The porcelain ones *I* bought in Dartmouth? The same porcelain knife handles we didn't know what to do with for ages, until, that is, *I* thought of displaying them in a frame? Is it those knife handles you're talking about?'

An irritable pause.

'That's not how I remember it. And anyway, it was *me* who framed them.'

I can't argue with this. It was him who framed them: badly, as I recall. But I don't tell him this because if I'm not very careful I will end up as petty as he is.

'And?' Although I know what is coming, of course.

16

'Since I'm coming over to pick up the engraving I might as well collect them at the same time.'

'Really?'

There is a surprised, possibly stunned, silence on the other end of the phone. He's not used to me showing any resistance.

'What's that supposed to mean?'

I find myself sighing again. 'Nothing. Okay, see you later.'

Then he's gone. Not even so much as a thank you.

I sip blackcurrant tea, close my eyes, get the usual picture in my head, am disturbed by it, afraid that I really am going mad. I open my eyes to rid myself of the image. I glance at the engraving again, think of the knife handles, of my grandfather clock, and all the other damn things Michael has taken from my house over the past few weeks, and I wonder where it will end. Will he keep on at me until he has taken everything? And when he's stripped the place bare, will he then take my house?

I stand up, pace around, rub my hands together distractedly. I picture myself on the street, like a character from a Dickens novel, turned out of my home, all my possessions given over to Michael.

I feel panicky. I can see it all now, what

Michael is up to, how clever and cunning he is.

I slump onto my chair again and put my hands over my face. The image is back, but this time it does not make me afraid. With sudden clarity, I know what it means. It has nothing to do with madness at all.

It is a sign.

A sign of what I must do to save myself from Michael's cunning and cleverness.

It's so damn simple, I can't imagine why I didn't think of killing him before.

Weedkiller and
Emporio Armani

I've just got back from Ilkley. Once my mind was made up I decided to get on with it straight away. Fortunately, *how* I would do it came to me very quickly. It came fully formed into my head as if it had been there all the time. Maybe it was there all the time and was just waiting for the right moment to be sparked into life.

They were very helpful in the wine shop but I didn't want to draw attention to myself in the gardening suppliers, so I just read a few labels and hoped for the best. It was a bit of a mad dash, because Nell phoned soon after Michael and told me she was coming over. I would have put her off if I'd thought of a good excuse quickly enough, but I didn't.

I haven't seen her for over a fortnight. She and David have been away somewhere nice. Venice, I think. She sent me a postcard but I threw it away after I read the message. I think there was a gondola on the front though, so it must have been Venice.

Nell has been great since my split with

Michael. I don't think I could have managed without her, in fact. Most of the people we called our friends are these days the friends of Michael and the typist, (or rather *ex-typist*, now, since Michael prefers his women in the home). They were very kind to me in the beginning, especially since I was considered the Injured Party. But Michael is so much fun and so outgoing and he won over our former friends with dinners and fine wines and in no time at all the ex-typist was accepted, and I became an embarrassment.

When Nell arrives, I make proper tea in a teapot and we drink it in the sitting room, with the early afternoon sun streaming in through the small-paned mullions. She tells me about her holiday with David. It was Venice. Venice, Rome and Florence. Nell isn't boring though, and she doesn't go on and on like some people do about their holidays.

When the joys of Italy in early summer have been adequately covered, Nell looks around the room and tells me how amazed she is by the amount of work I've done in the house, how it's hard to believe I've only been here a month. But then her eyes come to rest on a space by the window.

'Your clock,' she says, frowning. 'I knew something was missing.' She looks at me, waiting for an explanation.

I realise now why I was a bit unhappy about her visit. A lot has happened in a fortnight. Michael had removed a few things before she went away, but he's really been stepping up the pace recently. I try to think up some plausible lie to explain the clock's absence but I've never been very good at lying to Nell. So I tell her the truth instead.

She puts her head in her hand in a dramatic fashion. 'For Goodness' sake, Anna, where is it going to end?'

I know where it's going to end, of course, but I don't tell her. There are some things you can't even tell your best friend.

Nell is a very physical person. She works out a lot and it shows. Her skin always glows with good health. The only time mine glows is after a couple of whiskies. She puts down her teacup and gets up from her chair the way physical people do. There is nothing sluggish about Nell. She takes my cup from me and puts it down on the tray next to hers. 'Come on,' she says, 'up!'

So I get up from my chair the way people who aren't very physical and who don't like what they suspect is coming get up from chairs.

'Come on,' she repeats, and I follow her into the kitchen. She has her hands on her well honed hips as she looks around. 'Right,' she says, grabbing the memo pad and pencil I keep by the phone. 'Copper pots,' she says aloud, then writes it down on the paper. 'How many were there?'

'Ten,' I offer, and she looks at me with narrow eyes. 'Okay, fifteen.'

She shakes her head and adds the number to the pad. 'Now, what else has gone from here?'

I know I will get no peace till I've told her. I try to sound cheerful. 'The Worcester dinner service, oh, and some odd pieces of Delftware.' I don't mention the collection of glass rolling pins which she seems to have forgotten about.

We move into the dining room and the pencil hovers over the pad. 'Now, let's see,' I make a play of struggling to remember but I'm not fooling her. 'There's that collection of coloured glassware.'

'Venetian, wasn't it?'

I nod and quickly move on. 'Oh, yes, and that small display case with those old snuff boxes.'

'You mean those hand-painted enamel snuff boxes you took years to collect?'

I am beginning to feel very ashamed of my weakness, and more relieved than ever that I've made up my mind to do something about it.

She shakes her head again and adds the snuff boxes to her list.

Back in the sitting room, the list grows longer. 'But you know I never much liked them,' I say, when she notices the absence of a pair of Minton figures. 'I couldn't bear the silly expressions on their stupid little faces.'

She pulls a face which makes her look a bit like one of the figures. Then she starts looking around the room and like radars her eyes are drawn to the mule chest beneath the window. I bite my lip and wait for the reaction.

'Not the Okimono? Crikey, Anna, you could have lived for six months on what they would have fetched.'

Nell flops down in her chair and sighs. 'What am I going to do with you?'

I sit on the edge of my chair and wait while she studies her list, which takes a long time. I get the impression she is trying to tot up the value of the items but if she is then she's missing the point. The value doesn't matter to me, or it didn't, until I realised just what Michael was up to.

She finally looks up, and her eyes seem a bit glazed. 'It's got to stop, Anna, it really has. I honestly don't think we can get these things back now. Michael will just say they were gifts and I can't see you denying it.' She reaches for the teapot and pours warm stewed tea into her cup.

She sits back in her chair then and gives me one of her very serious looks, which makes me very uncomfortable. I get the feeling I'm in for some sort of psychoanalysis.

'You're absolutely right, Nell,' I say, before she can speak, 'I've been stupid.' I say this because experience has shown me that the quickest way to get someone off your back is to agree with them. And another good way is to be firm and positive. 'And I promise that it really will stop. He won't get another damn thing from me.'

'I hope you mean that, Anna.'

'I do.'

She does not look very convinced, but then she doesn't know what I know.

'I think it must be guilt,' she says, making a face at the contents of her cup before putting it back on the tray. 'You feel guilty for not giving him another chance.'

I sigh quietly, accept that assurances and acquiescence aren't quite enough for Nell, that she also needs reasons.

'But he was a pig to you, Anna, and you're well rid of him. What amazes me is that you didn't leave him years ago.'

If only it was as simple as she thinks it is. If only my life was as uncomplicated as Nell's clearly is. I don't know why I didn't leave Michael years ago, either, but I don't let him take my things because of guilt for not having him back. There's a lot more to it than that, but there really is no sense trying to work it out. Besides, it doesn't matter anymore. The important thing is that I've come up with a foolproof way of preventing him taking anything else.

So I carry on agreeing with Nell, tell her she's probably right about the guilt, that she's definitely right about Michael being a pig, and that yes, I was most certainly an idiot for not leaving him years ago. Which at last seems to satisfy her.

Then, in an attempt to change the subject completely, I tell her about the dance at the village hall.

'Sounds fun,' she says, 'I think I'll come with you.'

I groan quietly to myself. I hadn't bargained on that. I hadn't intended going at all, I just wanted her to believe I was making an effort.

'What about David?' I say.

'What about him? I don't have to get his permission to go out, you know.'

Pity, I think.

We talk a bit about other, inconsequential matters, then, just when I'm starting to get worried that she might stay longer than I want her to, she gets up and gathers her things together. She goes into the kitchen and pins the list she has made to my otherwise blank cork notice-board. It looks very accusing all by itself.

'I want you to promise to leave that list up there and look at it every time that creep rings you.'

'I promise.'

When she's gone, her perfume, Gio, lingers in the house, like a mother's dire warning never, ever, to speak to strangers. It lingers far longer than the list, which I hide in a drawer the moment she leaves; I can't risk Michael seeing it when he gets here. It might make him suspicious.

I check the kitchen clock: five past four. Still plenty of time.

★　★　★

For someone who has so many smile lines, Michael can be very cold. He is cold with me now as he enters my warm, cosy home. He is probably annoyed by its comfort. Annoyed that it is *his* money which provided the comfort.

I show him into the sitting room and it occurs to me for some reason that if it wasn't

26

for his baldness, Michael could pass for forty, though not thirty-five as he thinks he can.

He is wearing a suit from Emporio Armani which he bought in Manchester. I know it's from there because he doesn't buy his suits from anywhere else these days. He is proud of this fact. It started when he began his affair. New clothes are always a warning sign, I've since learnt. New clothes and new underwear, and he had lots of new underwear: drawers full of it.

I think he looks ridiculous in his Emporio Armani suit, especially since he has put on weight. It is in a style that footballers tend to wear when they're not playing football. Young men, not middle-aged idiots like Michael. The only other middle-aged men I have seen in this sort of suit are carpet wholesalers and men who own small chains of bookmakers.

'Would you like a drink?' I ask him, pleasantly.

He looks at me strangely. He looks at me for quite a while with those icy blue eyes of his, which makes me uncomfortable. I cannot help wondering if he is comparing me to the ex-typist, who is twenty years younger than I am. I've made a bit of an effort today, because Nell was coming, so I don't look too bad. I could never be described as pretty, but Nell insists I am still attractive; and although my body's not so firm as Nell's is, it's okay for my age. The way Michael is looking at me now though, makes me feel like a frump. Fair's fair, though. He thinks I'm frumpy and I think he is ridiculous.

'Half a glass of wine,' I suggest, 'while I fetch the knife handles.'

'I had hoped they'd be ready and waiting along with the engraving.'

Ah, the engraving. I don't say anything yet, though.

'Oh, go on, then,' he says ungraciously, as he casts his eyes over what remains of my possessions.

I go into the kitchen and collect the wine, which is already poured and mixed with weedkiller of the liquid variety, which, following a little experimentation, I found blended a lot better than the powdered kind. I went for a Chateau Beaucastle after explaining to the friendly wine-seller what I wanted, though not of course what I wanted it for. If it was going to disguise the weed killer, I knew that it must be full-bodied, but that's all I did know. I certainly had no idea it would be so expensive. Still, forty pounds will have been a small price to pay if this comes off.

I take the glass in to Michael. He is standing over my photograph table, frowning at the picture of my parents. I look at my father in his cheap wedding suit and if I had a knife in my hand now instead of this glass, I might be tempted to speed things up. He despised my parents, thought them beneath him, treated them badly.

He takes the wine from me and puts his lips to the rim of the glass. Of all the things I dislike about Michael, it is his lips I dislike the most. They are very thin and mean, cruel almost.

'It's a very good wine,' I tell him, then wish I'd kept my big mouth shut. Because now he's taken the glass away from his lips and is looking at the contents. He applies his nose to the full-bodied bouquet, and when he looks at me again his eyes are narrow.

Because the silence is uncomfortable, I start to babble. I tell him what it is, then how I came by it. 'A present from Nell,' I say, delivering the lie already prepared. 'For my last birthday. She's still trying to educate my palate. Can't seem to get it into her head that I go for quantity not quality.'

He raises a superior eyebrow, not at all amused by my little joke, but pleased by my admission of ignorance. 'A lost cause,' he says meanly. 'Wrong glass, as well. This is for white wine.'

Just for a moment there I thought he was

on to me. But I was wrong. he was just irritated to think I could afford to buy wines of such quality. I breathe a quiet sigh of relief.

'Nice gift,' he adds, but I can detect the criticism of Nell in his tone. He dislikes her for remaining loyal to me. She is also the only woman he knows with a greater knowledge of wine than he has, which is even more unforgivable.

'She says it has an unusual flavour,' I add, embroidering on my lie in case it tastes a bit odd.

'Smoked cherries, if my memory serves me correctly.'

Oh, bugger, I think. Trust him to know.

I watch the glass go up to his cruel lips again and I hold my breath. He sips, rolls the liquid around in his mouth, and swallows. He is frowning, which worries me. Ah, but no, what's that movement at the corner of his mouth, that look in his eye? I am reassured. It is definitely an expression of smugness.

'I was quite right,' he is saying, full of his own self-importance, 'smoked cherries it is.'

I am smiling as I leave the room. I take my time putting the badly framed knife handles in a cardboard box, and when I return the glass is empty. I pass him the box and he checks the contents.

'You've forgotten the engraving.'

'No, I haven't,' I reply. 'Or, at least, not that you wanted it. What I did forget is that it's being reframed. The old one broke in the move and I never much liked it anyway.'

The lie rolls easily from my tongue. The truth is I can see no point in giving it to him when he won't be around long enough to enjoy it. Besides, I have developed a sudden soft spot for the engraving and I don't want the ex-typist getting her sticky little mitts on it when Michael is dead.

He looks at me suspiciously.

'Don't worry,' I say. 'As soon as it's ready, it's yours.'

He shrugs. There isn't much he can say to this.

I watch him eyeing a pair of bird prints on the wall by the window.

'I don't want to keep you,' I say, when he seems in no hurry to go. I have no idea how long the weed killer will take to work and the last thing I want is him getting sick here.

He leaves without thanking me. Which is fine. It just makes me more certain I've done the right thing.

Cherubs and Ceilidhs

I get out the engraving and study it closely. Its meaning continues to elude me and it's making me very irritable.

It's Saturday now, nearly seven-thirty, and I am waiting for Nell to arrive. We are going to the ceilidh together and I am exhausted from trying to think up excuses of why I can't go, and worrying about Michael: about whether or not he is dead. I'm sure that he must be by now, but if he is, then why haven't I heard?

Now that I think about it, the engraving really could do with reframing. Maybe I'll get it done. Something a bit more dramatic than the plain black and gold wooden frame that it came in God knows how many years ago.

What the hell are those cherubs up to? — dragging and pushing that poor, flimsily-clad woman along through the wood. Not that she seems all that bothered. Now that I look a bit closer, I'm not even sure her expression is *enigmatic* at all. I think she is supposed to look that way but in fact she seems bored. 'Oh, go on then, take me wherever it is you're taking me, let's just get it over and done with.' That's what she seems to be saying, and the cherubs appear to be making very heavy weather of the job considering the woman is clearly putting up no resistance.

This is getting silly. How can a simple engraving I have barely noticed in years be the cause of so much frustrating speculation now? I despair with the thing and put it back in the kitchen drawer, where I hid it from Michael.

I think I might possibly spontaneously combust if I don't find out about Michael soon. It's been three days since he was here. He must be dead by now. He must.

I can stand it no longer. I have to find out, so I will just have to ring his house.

I dial my old number and the ex-typist answers in her silly, girlish voice. For once, Oasis aren't blaring out in the background, which I take as a good sign. Then I realise she sounds relatively normal, for her, which worries me a bit. She is supposed to sound upset. But maybe she's just a cold-hearted bitch.

'It's Anna,' I tell her.

I feel her coolness in the silence which follows.

'Michael isn't here,' she tells me, eventually.

Of course he isn't there, I think, but is that any way to put it? I hesitate for a moment, stuck for words. I can't say, 'Which undertakers is he at?' can I? That would really be giving the game away.

'He's going to be working late tonight,' she adds, which stumps me completely. Ah, but she must be having me on, I decide. She must be because today is Saturday and he never works at the weekend. It is sick, of course, but then I've always thought she was weird. Weird and stupid. Why else would she be living with a bald, middle-aged man with such appalling dress sense?

'He's been ill,' she volunteers, when I can think of nothing to say. 'So he had to go into the office today to catch up on some work.'

Oh God. She isn't joking.

'Ill, you say?'

'Yes, some sort of tummy bug. He was up all one night, vomiting, poor darling. I almost got the doctor out to him but he wouldn't hear of it. You know how brave he is.'

'Oh yes,' I say, 'he's always been very brave.'

I put the phone down and slide to the floor. Bloody, bloody hell.

★ ★ ★

Nell arrives looking gorgeous. She looks very Scandinavian with her pale, natural blond hair and her perfect skin. A bit of an ice maiden to look at, in fact, but not to know. She is incredibly warm and tactile, forever kissing and hugging. I put this down to her happy, uncomplicated childhood.

She hugs me now, tightly, and for some reason this makes me feel a bit sad. I pour Nell an orange juice, because she's driving and because her body is a temple, and a whisky for myself, because I need it. And while she's chattering on about her latest programme at the gym and how she's thinking about taking up jogging as well, I try to respond normally, though I feel anything but normal right now.

'You okay?' Nell is saying from a distance. 'You look a bit, I'm not sure . . . a bit strange.'

I shake my head, try hard not to look strange. 'Just worried about what I'm wearing, I suppose,' I say, glancing down at my plain tee-shirt and jeans. 'Maybe I should go and put on a skirt or something, like you.'

'You look fine as you are, terrific, in fact.'

I don't feel very terrific. I feel terrible. Sick to the soul with disappointment.

'Honestly, I mean it,' Nell persists. She has clearly mistaken my current low spirits for anxiety about the dance.

'And your hair looks really nice. You should

wear it up more often. You've got great bones and you should show them off.'

She's in annoying, Let's Boost Anna's Confidence mode, and the only way I will shut her up is to pretend that I am convinced. So I give her a cheesy grin, thank her, tell her she looks great too, which is true, and offer her another drink.

She glances at her watch. 'Don't you think it's time we got going?'

Since she thinks it's the dance which is top of my worries right now, I go along with it. 'I could do with a quick top up before I face a crowd of strangers.' I really could do with half-a-dozen to get over the shock of discovering Michael is still alive. The worst bit is that I keep getting an occasional jab at my conscience. Could I have made a mistake? Was messing it up a sign that I'm not supposed to kill Michael after all?

'Okay,' says Nell, 'but you don't have to worry. I mean, it's not as if you'll be on your own.'

I wouldn't have to go at all if you weren't here to make sure I do, I think unkindly. When I turn back with the drinks, I catch Nell's eyes circling the room, unable to resist checking to see if I've kept my promise. I haven't, of course, but since the knife handles were upstairs on the landing, I have a very good chance of getting away with it. I just hope she doesn't decide to visit the bathroom.

She takes her glass from me, raises it. 'To a fun evening,' she says.

I lift my own glass, force another smile, and try and think of something interesting to say, so interesting she might forget all about the ceilidh, which seems an even less attractive prospect than it did before my conversation with the ex-typist. Only Nell gets in first.

'Maybe there'll be someone attractive there tonight,' she says, giving me that look of hers, 'someone attractive *and* unattached.'

I groan to myself. Not that old chestnut. Not now. Nell has been trying to partner me off for the past six months and she still hasn't got the message. I'm just not ready for all that stuff. I don't think I'm cut out for it. I accept that all men are not like Michael, but knowing my luck I'll end up with someone just as bad. Or worse. So why take the risk?

But we've been through all this before, lots of times, so I give her an 'oh no, you don't' sort of look, and sip my drink. Then inspiration strikes.

'I had a call from Megan last week,' I tell her, and a genuine smile forms on my face at the thought of my daughter.

'How are things going for her?'

'Well, I think. She loves the job, anyway.' I glance at my photo-filled table. The most recent picture of Megan shows her on her twenty-first birthday; Michael and I were still together then, but only just. I know most mothers think their daughters are beautiful, but I believe that Megan really is. She took the best features of both her parents and none of the worst.

'You must miss her a lot. It's a pity she had to move so far away.'

'Even California is only a ten-hour flight these days,' I answer brightly. 'It used to take that long to drive to Cornwall.'

'True, but . . .'

I interrupt her. There is just a hint of criticism about Megan in Nell's tone, and I won't have that. 'It was me who encouraged her to go, Nell. This job was a great opportunity for her and besides, it isn't forever. She'll be back in a few months.'

'Still, Megan is your only real relative, and a daughter is very special.'

I think about this. Not about daughters being special, but the bit about Megan being my only relative. It makes me feel suddenly very alone. The sort of aloneness I felt when I was eight. When I made that momentous discovery.

My father was at work, and my mother was

in bed, sick, I think, and I was bored. So I did what most bored, eight-year-olds would do, I started poking into things which weren't supposed to concern me. It was the chance I'd been waiting for to look in the biscuit tin. It was a faded red tin with a scratched picture of the Houses of Parliament on the lid. The fact that I had been told not to touch it made it particularly attractive to me. It was kept, supposedly out of my reach, on the top shelf of a built-in, painted cupboard in the tiny sitting room that looked out over the potato plants and my yellow rose bush.

But I was a tall child for my age. Tall, and devious, apparently, because I remember putting the wireless on, to deaden the sound of the chair as I dragged it in from the kitchen, because I needed something to stand on. The tin was still just out of reach, so next I got the only book that was kept in the house, and put that on the chair. I remember that the book was a thick medical dictionary which my mother bought in a school jumble sale for a penny. God knows why. It was full of the most hideous, graphic illustrations of patients with disgusting diseases. It scared me witless, gave me terrible nightmares — but that day, at least, it was useful. It enabled me to reach the biscuit tin and, after a bit of a struggle, get it into my hands.

I think it took me about five minutes to realise why my parents didn't want me to look in that tin. I wasn't especially bright for my age but I don't think it would take any average eight-year-old long to realise what a Certificate of Adoption with their name on it meant. Any doubts were confirmed by my birth certificate. From that, I learnt the name of my real mother, but what intrigued me most was the blank where my real father's name should have been.

The funny thing is that I do not recall being shocked at the time. I accepted it without question. I had to, because I did not dare question my parents about it. But it complicated matters, this knowledge, which I had to keep to myself — this, and the fantasies which grew out of my secret.

I glance at Nell over my glass. And I thought she was supposed to be cheering me up.

'Sorry,' she says, apparently reading my mind. 'I didn't mean to depress you. But maybe it doesn't have to be that way. This could be just the right time to try and trace your real family.'

This feels a bit spooky. Is it possible that she really can read my mind?

'You've talked about it often enough,' she goes on, 'and who knows, maybe there's a

40

whole clan of them out there somewhere.'

Of course I've talked about it. Everyone who was ever adopted *talks* about tracing their blood relatives. But I've never done anything about it, probably because it always made me feel guilty about the people I thought were my parents until I was eight. But then they are both dead now.

'Maybe,' I say. 'Then on the other hand, I might find out things I'd sooner I hadn't.' I've grown out of the idea that my real parents were special. Fantasies like that are for children.

'But at least you'd know.'

Yes, at least I would know. Nell isn't going to let it drop until I say something else, so I say the only thing I can think of. 'I wouldn't know where to start.'

I suddenly realise that despite the fact that this conversation is keeping me from the dance, I am not enjoying it. It's making me very edgy. I'm almost relieved when Nell gets up and puts her glass on the drinks tray. 'What was your real mother's name again, by the way?'

'Brady,' I say, and I can see the name clearly now on the Certificate of Birth which I found in the tin with the scratched picture of the Houses of Parliament on the lid. 'Josephine Brady.'

I look up at Nell, but I am too preoccupied with the confused goings on in my mind to care why she's asking such questions.

And I have just realised something else. That the ceilidh, like death, is inevitable.

★ ★ ★

It is well into its swing when we get to the village hall. I am trailing Nell, who is supremely confident and always enters any room as if she is the star guest who everyone else has been waiting for. She looks around to see if she recognises anyone, not that it's likely being so far off her own patch. The only person *I* recognise is Helena Chopin and she, like everyone else in the room, is now performing horribly complicated steps to loud, jolly music. She spots me suddenly, waves frantically in my direction, like I'm her very best friend. Her face is red with excitement or exertion, or both. I lift my hand tentatively and return my own inhibited wave.

What the hell am I doing here?

Did I misread the signs about killing Michael?

Can these people really be enjoying themselves?

Should I try again or shouldn't I?

I look round for Nell and find that she's disappeared. I feel panic, like a child lost in a department store.

The dance is just coming to an end and as the lines of glowing bodies disperse, I spot Nell at the far side of the hall, and feel a ludicrous sense of relief. I watch her tap a dark-haired young man on the shoulder, and wait for him to turn and see her. She holds out her hands in the manner of someone who has just completed an impressive tap dance routine and is now waiting for her applause. After a moment of hesitation, the young man's face brightens into a wide grin of recognition, and Nell, who hugs everyone, hugs him.

When the hugging is done, he introduces her to his friends, and for a while Nell is centre stage: her natural position in life. Then the caller announces the next dance, and the group disappears behind a milling crowd of purposeful bodies.

I panic again for a moment, until I see Nell signalling for me to join her.

'I've found you a partner,' she announces when I've made my way through sweaty strangers forming squares of eight.

Six more strangers stare at me as I look at Nell blankly. She points me in the direction of the dark-haired young man she had made such a fuss of. 'Jack says he'll be happy to dance with you.'

'Jack Bailey,' he says. Then he grins at me, and I recognise that grin, only last time I'd seen it its owner's hair had been covered with something which looked like talcum powder. He looked a lot scruffier then as well.

I look fretfully at Nell. 'What about you?'

The caller begins explaining the moves.

'I'm partnering Jack's friend.' She looks at the tall young man next to her. 'Peter, isn't it?'

He nods and smiles at both of us.

I join Jack Bailey because I have no other option. To refuse now would draw even more attention to myself.

'Hello, Anna,' he says, showing me a set of bright white teeth. I can feel my face turning crimson as he takes my hands in his. They are the first male hands I have touched for ages.

The caller tells us the moves and it's clear Jack Bailey has done this sort of thing before. He pretends not to mind when I make a hash of the steps. 'Don't look so serious,' he says, 'this is meant to be fun.'

When the music begins I make an even bigger mess of the real thing. But gradually, I do begin to relax a little. I begin to concentrate, to forget about Michael, and by the end of the dance I am almost getting it right.

'Not bad for a beginner,' Jack Bailey says, winking at me, and I get that feeling in my stomach again.

Nell makes a Yee Hah! yelp at the end of the dance, which is quite inappropriate for English folk dancing, but everyone seems amused.

I'm still standing next to Jack Bailey when the caller announces the pie and pea break. I manage a smile, thank him for putting up with me, turn away, and come face to face with Helena Chopin.

'You'd better watch that young feller, love, he's got quite a reputation, you know.' She laughs, nudges me, ignores my red face, and introduces me to a small man whose name, she says, is Brian. She doesn't say what her connection with Brian is, but I get the impression he is her boyfriend or something.

Nell comes over and by now Jack Bailey has scarpered, off enhancing his reputation elsewhere, I expect. I do the polite thing, introduce Nell to Helena and Brian, and for the next few minutes the four of us chat about nothing much in particular. Then Helena says something about it being Brian's birthday soon and my mind starts drifting.

The two of them move off when the caller

advises us that the pie and peas are fast running out. Nell and I decide we can resist the temptation.

When we're alone again, Nell talks for a bit about dancing, about what good exercise it is, and how maybe I should think of taking it up seriously. She's always trying to get me to exercise.

'Well,' she says when she doesn't get any response, 'what did you think of Jack? Good looking, isn't he? Pity he's a bit on the young side, though.'

'He seemed very pleasant.'

'He did our extension for us. I'd forgotten he lived here.'

'He's a builder, then?' I say, thinking that would explain ceilings falling on him. 'That could be useful.'

'He's very good. Did a great job for us . . . Anna, are you listening?'

'Of course I am.' Which I have been, but only sort of, because mostly I've been thinking about something Helena said — about birthdays — and the idea it's given me, well half an idea, and it's the missing bit which has been taking up most of my attention.

I look up and see Jack Bailey heading our way, with Peter beside him. Nell sees them as well and nudges me.

I feel a bit irritated with her, then all of a sudden the thing I've been searching for comes to me.

I'm so pleased with myself that I forget to be shy and embarrassed and accept Jack Bailey's offer to partner me again with a smile. I feel genuinely cheerful as I step out onto the dance floor, my head full of new plans for getting rid of Michael.

Seaside Towns and Truffe de Calvados

If I still *want* to get rid of him, that is.

If I'm still *meant* to get rid of him.

That's what I'm trying to decide when I get home from the ceilidh. That's what I'm still trying to decide when I notice my answerphone flashing.

'Anna, this is Michael.' He sounds annoyed.

'I assume you're there, and are listening to this.'

How could he assume such a thing? I always take his calls. Presumably he can better imagine me being in and not answering the phone than he can imagine me going out.

A pause, as he is apparently still expecting me to pick up the phone.

'Okay.' (Irritated.) 'Shelly told me you tried to get hold of me today. Why?' (Heavy emphasis on '*why*'.)

Another long pause.

'Ah well.' (An attempt now at being pleasant.) 'I suppose you'll ring again if it's important. You can let me know then if it's okay to have those two bird prints, the ones I bought when we were on holiday in Kingsbridge.'

End of message.

'Salcombe, actually,' I tell the machine. 'And it was me who bought them. Bastard!'

I slump into my armchair and remember Salcombe. It was there, just over seven months ago, when we were celebrating our twenty-second wedding anniversary, that I found out about his affair.

I can recall only snatches of the period before my discovery. Our arrival at the hotel, drinking mead at a bar in the town, being battered by a November blast from the sea at South Sands, buying the bird prints from a shop in Fore Street. And I remember Michael's preoccupation, his lack of response to anything I did or said. Not that there was anything new about that, it was just more noticeable because we were alone.

It began to get clearer when we got back to the hotel on the last day of our stay. There was a message waiting for Michael at the reception desk. It was written on yellow notepaper, and had been carefully folded. He looked shifty when the receptionist gave it to him, and I remember the look that the receptionist gave me, which was nearly as shifty as Michael's.

I asked him about the note and he said it was *work*, that he needed to phone his office and that he'd do it downstairs. And I knew he was lying.

I knew it so well, that later, when he was taking a bath before dinner, I went into his jacket pocket and took out the note.

I unfolded the yellow notepaper slowly. I had a good idea what I was going to find, but did I really want to find it? Because once I had proof, there was no going back. I hesitated for a long time with the note in my hand. Then I heard the plug being pulled from the bath and I knew it was now or never. It was almost never. I actually got as far as folding the paper again, but then something happened. I saw myself ten years from now, into my fifties. I saw myself grey-haired and miserable.

So I opened the yellow notepaper again, read the words, felt . . . It is hard to recall my precise feelings. I remember that I was angry. I remember that I was frightened. I remember that I wanted to be sick. I remember that I wanted to punch Michael's face, beat it to pulp. But I cannot remember what I actually *felt*.

Missing you madly.
Ring me
Shelly.

I close my eyes, see those words again in my mind, and I realise that I'm not remotely confused anymore.

★　★　★

Nell rings the next morning to discuss the ceilidh.

'Good fun, wasn't it. We must do it again. What did you think of Jack?'

'I told you last night,' I answer wearily, 'I think he's very pleasant. And I'm sure he's an excellent builder.'

'I thought he might be a bit young at first, but he obviously liked you. I mean, he did dance with you most of the evening.'

'And Peter danced with you. Does that mean you are leaving David for him?'

'Anna, you're hopeless!' Then, thank goodness, she laughs. 'Okay, you win, this time. But I'm not giving up. I'll keep on nagging you until you agree to see someone.'

I can feel a big sigh coming on. 'You make it sound like there's a huge queue of eligible men outside my front door. Well, sorry to disappoint you, Nell, but there isn't.'

'There might well be if you'd open yourself up to the possibility.'

This is getting silly and I refuse to continue with it. 'Haven't you got some pressing exercise routine to attend to?'

'I can take a hint. Speak to you soon.'

★   ★   ★

I have one other very close friend. He is an elderly man who lives alone in a picture-book cottage next to a fast flowing river. He is an ex-neighbour of mine, although houses are so spaced out where I used to live that Harry's house is at least half a mile from my old home.

I visit him once a week, usually on Wednesdays, but I decide to bring it forward to Monday this week. Monday, 12th June. I rang him yesterday to make sure this was all right with him and it was.

He is an amazing man, is Harry. He has lived the past fifty of eighty-two years in the same house and although he has never travelled further than London (twice), he is one of the most open-minded and interesting people I have ever met. And his mind is incredibly sharp. He is the only person I know who can quote every one of Shakespeare's love sonnets by heart, for starters. He learnt them when he was in hospital recovering from his first heart attack, a couple of years ago. And he did it, he said, to prevent his brain going the same way as his body.

His crystal recall of past events is also extraordinary. It is the way he sees the events, however, that makes his recollections so entertaining. He is a lover of life and I envy his vision of the world. But the thing I love best about Harry is his integrity. He has the ability to restore my faith in humanity when it reaches rock bottom. I do not believe he has an underhand bone in his pleasingly rounded body. I trust him completely, and I wish I was not about to take advantage of the trust he gives back so freely to me.

He welcomes me with a hug. He is wearing a tweed suit and his old school tie — the local grammar, which is typical of his particular dress code. I have yet to see him in anything more casual.

His kitchen is shiny clean, and the green checked cloth on the table has been freshly laundered. There is a yellow rose in a vase in the centre, because he knows that they are my favourite. He makes tea for us both and produces scones he has made himself.

He gives the impression of a young man disguised as an old one, and although his movements are slow and deliberate, there is a vitality about him which is very rare. I tell him that he is wonderful, which I do all the time. I tell him this because it is true and because although he is a very special man, he, like all men, likes to be flattered.

I ask him how his book is going and he tells me 'Okay'. He has just mastered a word processor and is committing his memories to print. I assure him, as I always do, that it will be a bestseller.

'How are you, Anna?' he asks in his soft Yorkshire accent, as he passes me a cotton napkin. It is so neat and crisp that, as usual, I am almost afraid to use it.

I know this is not an idle enquiry.

'I'm good, as a matter of fact. I think I'm getting used to being alone.'

'Alone is fine, Anna. Lonely, isn't. You don't feel that, do you?'

I cut into the crumbly scone and look into his face. His eyes are no longer bright. They are clouded with age but they are eyes that see, really see. They see so well that it makes me nervous. I just hope he can't see what is going on in my head.

'I don't think so,' I reply brightly. 'Maybe sometimes, I suppose. I miss Megan, of course, and having the dogs around.'

He asks about Megan and I tell him about our latest chat on the phone. I tell him how happy she sounded, and how relieved I am that she's happy.

'She'll do well for herself,' Harry says. 'All that beauty *and* brains, she can't go wrong.'

I feel the usual pride when someone says something nice about Megan, and because it's Harry who's saying it, there is an extra glow.

We listen to the ticking of Harry's kitchen clock for a while, then he says: 'You should ask for the dogs back, Anna. They were always *your* dogs, and I'm sure they miss you as much as you miss them. They don't get nearly so many long walks as they used to.'

Harry would know about that, living so close to my old home.

I shrug, and spread pale creamy butter on both halves of my scone. 'I thought it was best for them staying here.'

'You thought it, or Michael did?'

I don't make any reply, I don't have to because we both know the answer to this already.

'I do have one problem, though,' I say, hating myself as I blurt it out.

'Oh?' Harry begins spreading butter on his own scone, a bit too thickly, as usual. 'Anything I can help with?'

'Well, yes, maybe. It's moles, I'm afraid. They're making a terrible mess of my lawn, piles of earth everywhere . . . ' I'm talking a bit fast as I do when I'm lying, so I take a deep breath and try to slow down. 'I thought about going to a garden centre for some advice.'

I bite into the scone and wait for him to suggest what I should do about it. He is a country man with country ways and I know he will not approve of me visiting a garden centre. He once told me his method of dealing with moles and although I know his memory is incredibly sharp I am hoping he can't remember everything he has ever told anyone.

'That's easy,' he says. 'I have just the thing. Remind me to give it to you before you leave. But you really must be careful how you use it.'

We talk then about the latest chapter of his book, which is about a loveable-rogue sort of poacher who was the bane of many a local gamekeeper's life.

I leave his picture-book house with a small glass bottle of strychnine and a heavy weight on my conscience.

★ ★ ★

I feel like a character from an Agatha Christie novel as I carve out tiny holes in the base of three *truffe de Calvados* and squeeze two drops of the diluted strychnine into each mushy centre. I'm using the dropper from my Bach Rescue Remedy. Harry told me he obtained the poison years ago, when it was still possible to get hold of poisons without too much trouble, about the same time that loveable-rogue was driving gamekeepers to despair. He assured me it will have lost none of its potency even after so long. He explained ever so carefully how I should use the strychnine to kill my moles. How I should dig up some earthworms and soak them in the diluted solution. How I should then dig a hole in the mole run and put the well soaked worms into the hole. It sounded horribly cruel to me. (As cruel as drowning kittens in a water tank, which my father did every time Tiddles, our cat, got pregnant, because that's how they dealt with unwanted animal pregnancies in the Irish countryside.) And I know for certain that if I really did have a mole problem that I wouldn't dream of getting rid of them in such a heartless fashion.

Once I've smoothed the carved out pieces back into place I am convinced that anyone would be hard-pressed to notice something amiss.

I feel dizzy with my badness. Michael loves

Marks and Spencer's French Collection of chocolates and *truffe de Calvados* are his absolute favourite. I had to go all the way to Keighley to get them, but it was definitely worth the effort. Michael will be delighted when they arrive for his birthday next week. And I needn't worry that the ex-typist will get her mitts on them — she may be a conniving trollop, but I don't think she deserves to die — because I know just how greedy Michael is.

It was Helena who made me think of birthdays and birthday presents, and it was Megan who reminded me that it was Michael's birthday next week. She talked about it when she phoned last week. She had decided not to send him a card, which means she still hasn't forgiven him for what's happened. For the affair, for hurting me, and for the fact that he is now living with someone the same age as she is. She hasn't spoken to him in ages, and says she won't set foot in her old home while the ex-typist is there. This is hard on Michael, I know, because he is fond of his daughter and because, like me, he is proud of her. But what's even harder, I suspect, is that while Megan continues to withhold her forgiveness, he believes that I am getting the better of him in an important sense.

When I've finished the job, I hide all the evidence at the back of my wardrobe and scrub my hands until they are raw.

The phone rings just before 'Coronation Street' is about to start. I hesitate before answering it then decide, damn it all, it can wait. Which is just as well. Had I taken the call I'm not sure how I would have handled it.

The message is brief.

'Hello Anna, this is Jack, Jack Bailey.'

A pause, then a slightly nervous cough.

'Um, well, I enjoyed meeting you that other night and I was wondering if maybe you would like to go out sometime? If you would like to, you can get me on the following number . . . '

I am completely astonished. So astonished, I switch 'Coronation Street' off and stare for ages at the answering machine. I play back the message to make certain I haven't imagined it. Apparently I haven't.

The end credits are rolling for the soap by the time I switch the TV back on, but I am still unable to account for a young, good-looking builder asking me out. I hardly even spoke to Jack Bailey between dances. What conversation there was had been dominated by Nell, which had suited me fine. I had been too preoccupied with methods of murdering my ex-husband to contribute much. Could he have mistaken this preoccupation for mystery? Is that why he phoned me?

Or was it Nell who put him up to it?

The more I think about this, the more likely it seems. I mean, she did go on about him quite a lot, didn't she. This thought makes me even more uneasy so I turn over to BBC 1 and 'EastEnders', and try not to think at all.

When 'EastEnders' is over, I pour myself a large measure of whisky and plan a letter to Megan. Guilt is a bugger. I'm feeling guilty now about murdering her father. It started with the memory of our telephone conversation about birthday cards, and despite an extremely exciting episode of one of my favourite soaps and a very unexpected answerphone message, it kept playing around in my head. Maybe I haven't thought this thing through properly. Maybe I should think it through now, think how killing Michael will affect his daughter.

So I do think about it, long and hard, with my hand paused over a blank sheet of paper.

When I'm finished thinking, I haven't come up with a single good reason not to kill him. Quite the opposite, in fact. Because while I was thinking, it occurred to me that if

Michael dies now Megan will be a wealthy young woman, whereas if he lives on, maybe marries the ex-typist, everything will eventually go to her. So in fact, I am really doing Megan a favour.

This cheers me no end. So I position my pen at the top of the page and begin to write. I tell Megan that I am well in the letter, that I haven't been this well for ages. I know this will please her, make her feel happier about being so far away.

The phone rings again just as I'm licking the envelope.

This time it is Michael, and I pick up the receiver when I hear his voice on the answerphone.

'Did you get my message?'

'Yes.'

And?

'Fine. I could drop them over if you'd like.'

'No need. I'll pick them up. How about tomorrow evening?'

I glance at the M & S chocolates, which I have yet to wrap, and realise I don't want him coming here. Not again. Not ever again. So I tell him a lie. I tell him I'm going out.

'Like I say, I'll drop them over to you sometime.'

I'm surprised when he accepts this without further protest.

'What did you want to speak to me about, by the way?'

I don't know what he's talking about for a moment, then I remember my brief conversation with the ex-typist.

'It wasn't important,' I tell him.

★ ★ ★

I can see why some women regard a visit to their hairdresser as therapy. Especially if their hairdresser is like Kevin. He's a tonic is Kevin, a fount of outrageous gossip, loads of fun, and a self-appointed guru of fashion. I love the gossip and the fun, but I find it hard to take seriously the fashion tips of a middle-aged man who squeezes his overly ample body into the latest and most flamboyant High Street gear.

Today, when I've listened to the latest gossip about one of Kevin's wealthy clients who ran off with a plumber, I tell him I would like a 'just got out of bed' look, which I think might suit me. This is meant to be a joke but Kevin is very enthusiastic. 'Just what you need, Anna. It will liven you up no end.' He tells me then that the hairbrush is the enemy of the *tousled* look and that I should throw mine away the minute I get home. He is all for extravagant gestures.

He trims my hair a bit on top and then makes me bend my head over my knees while he scrunch-dries it with a defuser. He is thrilled to bits with the effect. I'm not so certain, but I pretend to love it.

'It knocks ten years off you, Anna, for sure.' He calls his assistant over to give her opinion and she thinks more like fifteen. They seem so sincere that I begin to believe them, and if they are right, then that would make me just about the same age as Jack Bailey.

* * *

I rang him back just after I put the phone down on Michael. I rang him partly because of Michael. Because he expected me to be in whenever it suited him to call.

Jack Bailey seemed pleased to hear from me, just as Nell would be pleased when he rang to tell her about it. I should be mad with her for what she's done but I know she will have done it with the very best of intentions. In fact, now that I think about it, I find it all very reassuring. Had this been a genuine *date*, I would be in quite a state by now. Instead, I am surprisingly calm as I dress for the meeting.

We have arranged to meet in a pub in the next village. My suggestion, because I didn't want to start any local tongues wagging. He'd wanted to come here and pick me up but I needed to be more in control than that. If it isn't going well, I can make some excuse and leave in my own car.

Despite the fact that this is a set-up, I still take care to choose something to go with my new young image, created by Kevin: floaty skirt, fitted body, tailored lightweight linen jacket. Casual and smart at the same time. An outfit for all occasions.

I take trouble with my make-up as well. Foundation, mascara, lipstick, perfume. For me, the works. To finish me off, I put on some dangly earrings which are very nearly obscured by my *tousled* hair. (I can not bring myself to throw my hairbrush away, as I do not expect my new look to last very long.)

It is still light when I leave the house. It will probably still be light when I return. It is mid-June now, and I have known it to be light at eleven in mid-June, here in the north. And I do not expect to be out after eleven.

As I lock my front door, I pinch a yellow rose petal in my fingers, bruising it. I am disappointed by the absence of any scent on my fingers. My childhood rose bush had a glorious scent, which clung to my skin for ages.

I feel like a child now as I get into my

smart, grown-up car and start up the engine. I feel out of my depth. All my calmness leaves me as I set out for the pub where I have arranged to meet a young man with a reputation whose name is Jack Bailey.

I get to the end of the village street and stop the car. I can't do this, I realise. I just can't.

Bright Paper Packages and Long Lost Mothers

Jack Bailey rang twice last night, but I didn't pick up the receiver. He left messages on both occasions. In the first, which he left about half-an-hour after we were due to meet, he seemed only mildly concerned. He was wondering if maybe there had been some misunderstanding about the time, and that he hoped, since I wasn't in, I was now on my way.

The next call came an hour or so after that. He sounded fed up this time.

'It was meant to be tonight, wasn't it? Anyway, I'm going home now, but give me a call when you get this, let me know what's going on.'

I nearly did, as well. I felt really bad about him waiting in the pub for me all that time. I rehearsed some lies in my head about getting delayed somewhere, but then I got worried in case he suggested we try again, make some new arrangement, so I decided against it. After the second message I switched off the lights, in case he passed the house on his way home.

What surprised me is that I didn't get a call

from Nell. I was sure she would ring and tell me off for being such a coward, but then maybe she doesn't want me to know about her involvement.

I didn't sleep too well last night so I got up very early and cleaned the house. Really cleaned it. I felt a bit sad at one stage, when I realised that dog hairs were no longer a problem — and to think how I used to curse when they were. But I kept at it, because I needed something to take my mind off the new doubts which kept creeping into my mind. I even cleaned out the oven, which I haven't done since I moved here. Not that it really needed it. I tend to do most of my cooking in the microwave these days: pre-packed dinners for one.

Anyway, it did the trick nicely. It's true what they say about physical labour being the cure for an uneasy mind.

So now, my house spotless, I wrap up the box of Marks and Spencer's chocolates in shiny red paper and tie it with silver ribbon. It takes ages to do this in my rubber gloves.

Michael has lots of friends and business acquaintances who send him birthday gifts, and he will probably assume that whoever sent the chocolates simply forgot to enclose a card. He will hardly give the matter a thought.

I put the package in a brown padded envelope and disguise my handwriting when I address it. Neat, bold, unidentifiable capital letters.

I think about posting it along with Megan's letter in the village, but decide it will be safer to take it to Ilkley. Before I leave the house, I put what remains of the red shiny paper and silver ribbon in a plastic bag. I will dispose of them in an anonymous bin somewhere.

An early mist has cleared and the air is warm. Too warm for the jumper I'm wearing, the same scruffy jumper I did all the cleaning in, but I cannot be bothered to change now. I toss my bags in the car and start it up. At the far end of the village I notice a dark-haired young man getting into a white van. It's a moment before I realise who it is. A bit late, I put my hand up to the side of my face and hope Jack Bailey doesn't know what kind of car I drive.

I do what I have to in Ilkley, and when I've done it, I feel quite light hearted and decide to wander around the town for a while to fill in some time. It's looking its usual pristine self, with masses of brightly coloured flowerbeds stretching the length of its wide-paved main street. It is a very smart town, inhabited by smartly dressed people, and I feel very out of place in my scruffy jumper and jeans.

What I like best about Ilkley is its dramatic backdrop. I love the stark contrast of the high, wild moor with the town's quiet gentility. Ilkley Moor, best known for its health-giving well, for the famous rugby song it inspired, and more recently, for its high number of UFO sightings.

In one of the town's smart shops, I buy a book on caring for roses, and in another, a poster of a sun drenched lemon grove, for my bathroom. I have been looking for one like it for ages and I cannot believe my luck. It is a very good sign. It means that I have done the right thing in sending those chocolates to Michael.

★   ★   ★

Home again, and the poster Blu-Tack'd to my bathroom wall, I decide to ring Jack Bailey. The glimpse I had of him earlier has made me realise how likely I am to bump into him sooner or later, and how embarrassing that will be if I don't attempt some kind of apology.

I expect him to be out. I took special note of the fact that the white van was gone as I passed through the village on my way home.

I also took note of the house I think must be his, a neat little terraced cottage with hollyhocks growing by its front door.

I am shocked when he answers the phone. So shocked I can't reply when he speaks. The plan was to leave a well rehearsed message on his answerphone. But the voice which answers is the real thing.

'Jack Bailey,' he repeats, 'is anyone there?' He sounds out of breath, as if he's just got back and had to run to answer the phone.

'It's Anna,' I say, in a voice which does not sound much like my own. I would have put the receiver down but it occurred to me that he might do a 1471 on me and then I would look an even bigger fool.

There is a brief pause, then, 'So what happened to you?' He doesn't sound cross, just interested.

Because I am off-balanced by finding him in, I forget the excuse I've prepared and blurt out the truth. 'I nearly came,' I said. 'I got to the end of the village then, I don't know why, but I just couldn't go any further. You must think I'm mad.'

'I don't know about mad. A bit rude, maybe. You could have phoned to let me know.'

'I know, I'm sorry. I should have.'

'So that's it, then?' he says. 'You don't want to see me?'

'It's not that, I mean . . . '

What do I mean?

I take a deep, calming breath, and feel even more confused.

'Look, Anna, I don't know what's going on in your head, but it's all very straightforward as far as I'm concerned. I like you, I thought we might have something in common, so I asked you out.' He sounds just a little bit cross now.

'But it isn't that simple,' I tell him. 'You must have noticed I'm quite a lot older than you are.'

'Is that what's bothering you?'

'Well, yes, that and . . . Oh, it doesn't matter.' I'm squeezing the receiver so tight my knuckles must be white.

'And what?' he persists.

'And the fact that Nell put you up to it. I thought I didn't mind at first, but I do. It makes me feel like a charity case.'

I hold the phone away from me when I hear him chuckle. I can't believe it. I can't believe he thinks that this is a laughing matter.

'You've got it all wrong, Anna,' he says when he's finished chuckling. 'Nell didn't 'put me up' to anything. I haven't even spoken to her about you. And yes, since you mention it, I have noticed you're older than I

71

am but I wouldn't have called if that mattered to me. So if that's all that's worrying you . . . '

Of course it's not all that's worrying me. If Nell really wasn't behind this then clearly this has something to do with his famous reputation. Maybe he thinks being seen with an older woman will add to it. I think this but I don't say it. I reckon I've said more than enough already.

'How about giving it another go?' he says then, and because I can't think of any more objections I care to admit to, I find myself agreeing.

'But not till next week,' I tell him.

'Fine, how about Wednesday evening, at eight? Only this time I'll pick you up if you don't mind.'

'Okay,' I reply, and then I remember that Tuesday is Michael's birthday, and that by the time Jack Bailey comes to my house on Wednesday, he will almost certainly be dead.

★   ★   ★

I look back at the last few days with some satisfaction. To stop me thinking about things, I decided to decorate my bedroom, which I've been planning to do since I moved in. It was quite a big job. I started by stripping the old pink flowery wallpaper with a steam machine, which was so effective it removed three patches of plaster as well. I panicked for a while when this happened, and very nearly called Nell. I even thought of calling Jack Bailey for advice but decided against it. I didn't want him getting any wrong ideas.

So I sat down in my kitchen and drank coffee, which I hadn't done for a while, and suddenly realised what had to be done. I would consult *Yellow Pages.*

Three plasterers were out, but the fourth replied straight away. I was lucky to catch him in, he said.

I told him that it was urgent and he was at my house within the hour. He was an odd little man, the size of a steeplechase jockey, with a voice to match.

He eyed up what had to be done and said it would only take half an hour if I wanted him to do the job straight away. So I made him coffee and listened to him talking about folk music and playing the bodhrán. He even sang a few verses of 'Peggy Gordon' to me which was a bit embarrassing, though he actually had quite a good voice. I got the impression that he was really quite lonely.

When he left, thirty pounds better off, I felt ludicrously pleased with myself. I realised how well I was coping with life on my own. I could buy a house, use a steam wallpaper stripper, and I could sort things out when they went wrong.

★   ★   ★

I am feeling very cheerful when Harry rings. It is Monday morning, and my bedroom is finished, a vision now, I like to think, in lemon and pale green. It is like a spring garden.

I have just arranged yellow roses in a vase for the kitchen table and I am pleased with the effect. Once I'd finished decorating on Sunday evening, I read a bit of my new book about caring for roses. It told me it was good to cut the blooms now and then to allow for new growth, so that's what I've done.

'How are the moles faring,' Harry asks, and I feel my face colour. I'm just glad he can't see me. I tell him I've followed his instructions to the letter and await their imminent destruction, little horrors.

'I'm ringing to ask you a favour,' he says then.

'Anything, Harry.'

'You haven't heard what it is yet.' A pause, a pleasant little laugh, then: 'The thing is, Anna, I'm finding it hard to cope with this damn word processor, and I wondered if you could spare the time to do some typing for me.'

'I'd love to, but I thought you'd mastered the *damn* thing by now.'

'Oh, I can work it, all right, it's just that I find my thoughts don't flow very well when I'm using it. They come out better on paper, but then it takes so long to type everything up afterwards. And I'm beginning to worry that I might never get it finished.'

I am a bit annoyed with him for saying this, or rather annoyed by the implications of what he's saying. I know what he means. He means that he might not be around long enough to get the book finished, which is silly. But I don't let my annoyance show. 'When do you want me to start?'

'Would tomorrow be all right?'

'Tomorrow's fine. See you then.'

Tomorrow, the 20th June, is Michael's birthday.

When I put the phone down, I see that there are three letters waiting on the doormat for me. A gas bill, a letter from Megan, which will have crossed with my letter to her, and one from someone whose handwriting I do not recognise. I ignore the bill and read Megan's letter while I drink blackcurrant tea and wait for my porridge to cook in the microwave. I have drunk far too much coffee

75

over the weekend and I'm trying to be good again. New week, fresh start.

Megan seems happy. She spent the day before writing the letter at Venice and has gone into great detail about the strange and wonderful sights to be seen there. She was nearly persuaded to get a tattoo (she doesn't say on which part of her anatomy), but that good sense prevailed in the end. I smile at this and heave a small sigh of relief.

She writes that there is more to Venice than the eccentrics who are drawn there, and how she spent an hour or so being guided around the canal system which makes it look a little like the place it was named after. '*A Hollywood version, anyway. Quite charming, really.*'

She mentions the restaurant she ate in, just off Santa Monica Boulevard. A place lots of famous people hang out in, usually, only she didn't see anyone famous that night. '*Just my luck!*' she wrote, but she does not seem all that disappointed.

She leaves it till the end of the letter to tell me who she did all these things with. '*He's wonderful*', she wrote about someone called Brandon. '*He's works for the same company I do and I think he might just be The One*'.

I do not take this very seriously. Megan has met The One a couple of times before and then it turned out that they weren't The One after all. For the moment I'm just glad that she's happy.

The microwave pinged ages ago, and when I take my porridge out it is only just lukewarm. I add some honey and stir it into the glutinous mess. It's not easy being sensible about eating.

I wonder if Michael's chocolates have arrived yet. Of course they will have, I assure myself. I sent them first class. They will have arrived ages ago. But he won't have eaten them yet. He never opens his gifts before his birthday.

I can picture the scene tomorrow morning, in the kitchen that was once my kitchen. Surrounded by all his much prized convenience gadgets, Michael will be seated at the table. By now he will have instructed the ex-typist how he likes things to be on his birthday, just as he instructed me. And the first thing I learnt is that he likes his presents piled high. Presents are very important to Michael.

I remember how mad he was with me at Christmas when I didn't send him a gift. He phoned me on Christmas Day to tell me what a bitch I was. I thought that was rich considering everything that was going on at the time. But he'd sent me a plant, a seasonal poinsettia, through Interflora, and couldn't for the life of him understand why he hadn't received anything from me. I was living in a cheerless second-floor flat in Ilkley at the time, and I threw the bloody thing out of the window. I didn't even look to see if anyone was walking past.

I open the other letter, the one with the handwriting I do not recognise. I have already tried deciphering the postmark, but it has been badly stamped and I cannot make it out. The letter is short and written with a fountain pen which strikes me as being unusual. Who do I know that uses a fountain pen?

The handwriting is remarkably clear but I still cannot make any sense of this letter. It claims to be from a Josephine Brady, who says she gave birth to me forty-four years ago. She says she is pleased that I wanted to get in touch with her, that she hoped I would one of these days. She says she does not want to go into too much detail about herself now, just in case I have second thoughts about everything. She is leaving it up to me.

I look at the address at the top of the page and see that Josephine Brady (or Josephine Brown, as she is now) lives in Solihull.

I am remarkably calm as I fold the letter and put it back in its envelope.

I pick up the telephone receiver and dial Nell's number. I know exactly who I have to thank for this.

'I can't believe it!' she squeals, then hardly pauses again for breath. 'I only got onto the detective agency last Monday. They said it should be easy enough but I never dreamed they'd be *that* quick. I suppose they should have warned me really, then I could have warned you. But not to worry. Isn't it absolutely brilliant, Anna! She must have been thrilled that you've made contact after all these years.'

I feel numb. I know I should be feeling some proper emotion, but I don't know what it should be.

'Except it wasn't me who made contact with her.'

There is quite a long silence, then, 'Oh God, Anna, you're not pleased, are you?'

'I don't think I am, no. Why did you do it, Nell, without discussing it with me first?'

'I thought you'd be happy, I really did. I thought it was what you needed.'

I can hear the hurt in her voice and I want to make it all right for her, but since it isn't all right with me, I can't.

'Like you think I need a man in my life. Nell, you're a good friend, but it isn't up to you to decide what's best for me.'

'I feel terrible. I'm sorry. You're right, I shouldn't have done it. I shouldn't be trying to organise your life. Are you very upset?'

'I'm not sure how I feel just at the moment. I need time to let all this sink in.' It's hard to stay mad with Nell when she's being so contrite.

'Shall I come over?'

'No, don't do that. Like I say, I need some thinking time.' I'm about to put the receiver down, when I remember. 'I'm sure tracing long lost mothers doesn't come cheap. You'll have to let me know how much I owe you.'

'Oh, Anna, please don't say that. It was intended to be a gift.' A hurt pause, then, 'Look Anna, if you don't want me there today, that's fine, I understand, but I shall come tomorrow evening, about eight. We have to talk about this.'

When I put down the phone, I go into the sitting room, look at the photograph of my beaming parents, and feel over-whelmed by the guilt I always knew I would feel if this thing ever happened. Then I sink into my chair, put my head in my hands, and try to cry. I make all the noises but I can't seem to squeeze any tears out. Maybe I've got blocked ducts or something. I've been trying to cry for ages now and I still can't manage it.

Strong Coffee and Silver Cardboard Keys

It's the morning of Michael's birthday, and although it is only 7.00 a.m., I have been up for ages: drinking coffee, wandering around the house, listening and trying not to listen to the clatter going on in my head.

I think I have made a terrible mistake. About sending those chocolates to Michael. And I think it's that letter from Josephine Brown, née Brady, which has made me realise how big a mistake it was. Despite the hard time I gave Nell, despite feeling guilty about the people who brought me up, I can't help feeling hopeful. I can't help wondering what my mother is like, and if I am like her. And if Michael dies, and I am sent to prison for years and years, I might never know.

Once I'd got that clear in my mind, I started to realise other things. I know now that I was kidding myself when I decided I was doing Megan a favour. I mean, how is she going to feel when she hears that her father is dead, killed by her mother, and she didn't even send him a birthday card? She will be distraught. She will never forgive herself.

And then there's Harry. How's he going to feel when he finds out that his poison killed Michael?

So I have to undo what I've done, which is why, for the last hour or so I have been waiting for the right time to ring Michael. I know it is going to sound odd, but I am just going to have to tell him it was me who sent the chocolates, but that he is not to eat them. I shall try to avoid telling him why he is not to eat them, but if needs be then I shall just have to come clean and face the consequences, which will be far lesser consequences than if he ate them.

So now, I take a deep breath, pick up the receiver and dial Michael's number. My heart is racing as I listen to the ringing tone: three, four, five rings . . . eighteen, nineteen, twenty. Where the hell is he?

I replace the receiver, look around the room, which is beginning to spin. I wonder if I am going to faint, but I can't faint now, I've got things to do. If Michael isn't answering his phone, then I am just going to have to go to the house.

I run upstairs, get dressed, get into my car and drive, very fast.

The first thing I notice when I pull up

outside my old house is that the dogs are not barking. And they always bark when a car pulls up. The next thing I notice is that Michael's car is not in the drive. And he always used to keep it in the drive overnight, for a fast getaway in the morning.

I ring the doorbell and when no one answers, I nip round the back of the house and peer through the kitchen window. Nothing. No presents piled on the kitchen table, no sign of life at all. I glance at my wristwatch, seven-thirty, just about the time Michael normally has his breakfast. This makes no sense at all.

I move on to the dining-room window, wonder if they've changed the tradition, have breakfast in there now, but there's nothing. Nothing in the sitting room either, or in Michael's study. It is a bloody mystery.

I think about breaking in, but since I can't see the presents through any of the windows there doesn't seem any point. And besides, if he isn't home, as the missing car seems to suggest, he must have gone to work early, and if he's at work he can't be stuffing his face with *truffe de Calvados*.

Which gives me some breathing space.

If I go on now to Harry's, do some work for him, maybe I can come back later, when I'm a bit calmer, when there *is* someone in, when the ex-typist is back from walking the dogs, which, since neither she nor they are around, she must be doing.

★ ★ ★

If Harry is surprised by my early arrival, he doesn't say so. He's cooking his breakfast when I get there, a huge fry-up, which he offers to share with me. I settle for a cup of fresh coffee. I have already blown my good intentions regarding caffeine, so another cup isn't going to make much odds.

Harry eats his breakfast and I drink my coffee in silence. That's another good thing about Harry. You don't have to keep trying to think of something to say all the time. He once told me that he thought people were afraid of silence, and I think he is right.

I am glad of this silence. It's giving me time to get my head straight, think about how I'm going to get those chocolates back. If I'm not too late, that is. No, I daren't think about that. Only I can't help thinking about it. I mean, what if Michael broke the habit of a lifetime and opened the chocolates last night? What if he's in hospital at this very moment with a team of doctors trying desperately to save his life? I looked up strychnine poisoning in my general encyclopaedia and found that it is a very grisly business; it didn't mention anything about antidotes. I would need a more specialised book for that kind of information.

'You look absorbed, Anna,' Harry says when I put my empty cup down. (Is it possible that he is afraid of this particular silence?)

'Do I? I was thinking about my bedroom,' I lie. I tell him how it is now lemon and pale green, and about the tiny plasterer who sang a couple of verses of 'Peggy Gordon' to me. Harry loves a bit of a story, so I exaggerate a bit and make the plasterer even smaller and the holes he had to fill in even bigger.

I do not tell him about Josephine Brown because Harry does not know that I was adopted. I have not deliberately withheld this from him, it's just that we don't talk about that sort of thing. I'm not sure why.

He is duly amused by the blown up version of my wallpaper stripping catastrophe, then, quite out of the blue, he says:

'Did you know Michael is away at the moment? Gone off somewhere for his birthday.'

I like the way Harry never refers to the ex-typist, though I know he means they have both gone away. Then it hits me, what he's said.

'Did he say where he was going?' I ask, just for something to say really, while my mind is buzzing.

Harry shakes his head. 'No, just that he would be away for a week, and that he's put the dogs in kennels.'

★   ★   ★

At one o'clock I make up my mind to leave. I intended working longer but I've made so many typing errors that I can see no sense in continuing. While I did work, Harry plied me with coffee and biscuits and openers for my opinion about his stories. I told him I especially liked the one about the old woman from a remote Dales village who grew loofahs in her greenhouse, which is the only thing I could actually remember. The rest could have been the Old Testament for all the attention I gave it. It was just words, words I kept getting wrong. All I could really think about was Michael, on holiday somewhere, with a box of poisoned M & S French Collection in his suitcase.

'You must have some lunch before you leave,' Harry says, and although I refuse, I do accept a cup of tea. All that coffee has made me thirsty.

He brings out his special-occasion blue

china pot, then he turns back to the dresser and takes a flat, see-through box out of a cupboard. He opens the box and arranges some of its contents on a doily-covered plate.

'A bit of a treat,' he says as he puts exotic-looking chocolates in front of me.

I feel the blood drain from my face as I look at them. M & S French Collection, if I am not very much mistaken. My voice is shaky when I speak, but I don't think he notices.

'Nice, Harry, a present?'

'From Michael, as a matter of fact,' he says turning from me again to get plates — not that you need plates for chocolates.

'He dropped them in last night,' he goes on, glancing over his shoulder, 'when he told me he was going away. Said he was on a diet and would I like them? And you know me, Anna, never could look a gift horse in the mouth.'

Christ Almighty, I think. 'Don't blame you,' I say.

He turns back to me and puts blue plates on the table. They go with the teapot.

I am at a loss for words as I watch him manoeuvre himself carefully on to his chair, opposite me. I'm looking at the chocolates on the doily-covered plate, all six of them, and trying to make up my mind whether one of them is a *truffe de Calvados*. I decide that one is. Just one, thank God.

I grab it from the plate and as I make some remark about noticing how Michael had put on weight last time I saw him, I examine the bottom of the chocolate for signs of interference, and find it. I can just make out part of my thumb-print, where I'd moulded the chocolate back after scraping it out.

'He didn't seem much different to me,' Harry says, taking a *choc au citron* from the plate. I watch it going towards his mouth. Yes, it is definitely a *choc au citron*.

As he takes a small bite, I make a play of popping the *truffe de Calvados*, whole, into my mouth but, with what I hope is a clever sleight of hand, slip it instead into my cardigan pocket. I pretend that my mouth is stuffed with delicious chocolate and Harry, being such a gentleman, does not look at me. I make greedy noises and dive in for another one which tastes of marzipan. It is disgusting.

All the time I am wondering how I am going to get the rest of those chocolates away from Harry. Then I remember something I heard once about desperate situations calling for desperate measures.

So I get up and go round to the box. It's not me, this, but Harry is rarely surprised by anything and is far too generous to object when I ask if I can have the other two *truffe de Calvados*, which I tell him I simply adore.

'Of course you can have them, Anna. Take the box, if you like. I'm not really all that fond of chocolate, anyway.'

'Okay,' I say, thinking that it is better to be safe than sorry.

I put the see-through lid back on the box and slip them into my black and red woven duffle bag which is hanging on the back of Harry's chair, where I left it.

I drink my tea in one go, while I am standing, then tell Harry I really must fly but that I will see him again tomorrow.

And Harry, who is rarely surprised, has a look of surprise on his face as I plant a kiss on his whispy-haired head, and make a hurried escape.

★ ★ ★

I have a very silly thing amongst my possessions. It is a silver cardboard key, about a foot long. Attached to it is a spray of twisted fabric flowers, a black cat — for luck, and just for good measure, a silver horseshoe, as well. There is a chrome bar amid all this paraphernalia. When it is wound up it plays a tinkly version of 'Happy Birthday To You'. It still works after all these years.

My parents gave it to me for my twenty-first birthday. This, and a set of three china swans of varying size. I have no idea where those swans are now.

It shames me to remember that birthday, and the party to celebrate it. It was Michael who suggested the party, and I was flattered to be made such a fuss of, especially since we hadn't known one another very long at the time. He went ahead and organised everything, the hotel, the food, the drinks, the invitations.

There was no question of inviting my parents. I should have known, really. I should have known by his reaction when I introduced them to him. He'd been shocked by their home and their humble ways.

There were about one hundred and fifty people at the party in all, of which I knew about four really well. It didn't feel much like a twenty-first birthday party, more like a networking exercise for Michael's business ambitions. I don't think I enjoyed it very much, I can hardly remember it now, but I do remember that later, when the party was over, that I hated myself.

Why I am looking at this key now as I am waiting for Nell to arrive, I'm not sure. I suppose it must have something to do with Josephine Brown's letter.

And the guilty mind works in mysterious ways.

★   ★   ★

Despite my change of heart, I still don't feel ready to talk about Josephine Brown to Nell. I'd prefer to watch my soaps, try and forget everything for a while. But it's too late to stop her coming now, so I put the cardboard key away in my desk and pour myself a glass of chilled wine.

I watch the start of 'Coronation Street' as I sip my wine, and try to concentrate on a riveting plot which looks as if it may very well lead to the death of one of the Street's most popular characters. I try, but it's hard.

The doorbell rings just when the advertisements begin at the end of part one. Nell, I assume, has come early. I switch off the television and grudgingly answer the door. I am surprised, no — I am amazed, to see Hilary Davidson standing on my doorstep.

'Anna!' she gushes. 'How wonderful to see you.'

I wish I could say the same. I look to see where her car is parked and if she's alone. I see it under a tree a few yards away and note, with relief, that there's no one else in there. Hilary and Raymond would have been just

91

too much. Hilary on her own is too much, as it is.

'Well,' she says, 'aren't you going to invite me in?' She is already moving towards me and I step back and let her pass. Hilary Davidson is famous for her pushiness and I am too surprised by her appearance to put up any resistance. She is in the sitting room, looking around. I can tell she is unimpressed.

'I can't stay long,' she tells me, and I thank heaven for small mercies. 'I'm on my way to an eight o'clock meeting at your village hall on the future of our National Park. I wondered if you were going along?'

I am surprised at this. I wouldn't have thought that conservation was Hilary's thing. I shrug, tell her no, that I didn't even know there was such a meeting and she looks sorry for me.

'Not integrated yet into the local community? Still, give it time.'

She looks at my glass of wine but I do not offer her any. I do not even ask her to sit down but she sits down anyway, on *my* chair.

As usual she is dressed up like a dog's dinner: high heels, short skirt, padded shoulders, lots of gold jewellery. I wonder why she has bothered to come here. I haven't seen or heard of her since long before the divorce.

'Raymond and I were at Michael's birthday party on Saturday,' she tells me, 'before he and Shelly went off on their marvellous holiday to the Florida Quays.'

Ah, so that's where they've gone, and that's why Hilary is here. She has come to gloat.

'It was a marvellous bash. Shelly really excelled herself. Oh, sorry, Anna, I suppose I shouldn't have said that, should I?'

'Why not?' I say, 'if it's true.' Though I doubt very much that it is true. From what I have heard about the ex-typist, I would be surprised if she could organise a séance in the proverbial mortuary. But Hilary isn't listening.

'We played all sorts of silly games but it really was fun, and the food was excellent. I insisted that Shelly gave me the name of the caterer.'

When she is not examining her long fingernails, she keeps darting glances at me, trying to gauge my reaction. She is probably wondering why I don't sit down. I don't sit down because I don't want her getting comfortable. I don't want her thinking she can call in here when she feels like it.

'How are things going with you, Anna?' she asks in a deeply sympathetic tone that makes me want to punch her.

'Fine,' I say. I would like to add that life is

incredibly wonderful, that I have rampant sex every day with a series of passionate lovers, anything to take that pitying look off that overly made-up face.

'Do you know, Anna, I didn't realise it at first, but Shelly is the very image of Kim Basinger. Well, a young Kim Basinger, with dark hair, of course.'

Christ! I think. You silly, silly cow. Is there anyone you know who isn't the very image of some celebrity? According to Hilary, Michael is a dead ringer for Pierce Brosnan — without the hair; Raymond, her own puny husband, bears a striking resemblance to Harrison Ford — without the muscle tone; and she, herself, is an exact Jerry Hall look-alike, lacking only the height and the long hair. Apart from that, they are as twins, apparently, right down to their perfect size eight figure and their belief in firm parenting.

In the old days she used to compare me to Cher — before all her plastic surgery, of course.

I look pointedly at my wristwatch. 'Five to eight,' I tell her, rudely, 'your meeting will be starting soon.'

I make for the door and because she is too surprised to protest, she gets up and follows me out.

'Kind of you to call in,' I tell her. 'Do give

my best wishes to' — I almost say Harrison, but resist — 'Raymond.' I do not make any of the usual meaningless, insincere offers, like 'You really must come around together sometime,' because she might take me up on it. I just close the door on her and breathe a sigh of relief.

Sex and Blue Conifers

Nell is wearing jeans and a tee-shirt, thank God. I could not have stood another glamorous woman in my house tonight.

When she's hugged me, apologised again for interfering in my life, I tell her about Hilary, and we laugh about the latest addition to her look-alike Hall of Fame.

It's strange, but Hilary's visit has had an effect on me. Not a bad effect, either. In fact, I feel strangely pleased with life, though I'm not at all sure why.

'Kim Basinger after a round with Mike Tyson,' Nell says, cruelly, and I love her for it, especially since I have a fairly good idea that the ex-typist is actually quite pretty. Pretty, but thick.

I pour more wine for myself and a glass for Nell, glad now that she's come despite my earlier misgivings. We giggle some more about Hilary-stupid-Davidson, then, when we exhaust the whole nonsense of it, Nell asks me about Megan and I tell her about her latest letter and about someone called Brandon, but not the bit about him being The One. I'm a bit worried about that, as a matter of fact. I'm not sure if I like the idea of her falling in love with a man who lives six thousand miles away.

Nell doesn't have any children. She and David tried for a while, but mainly because they thought it was the thing to do. I don't think either ever felt a deep need for a child. Not the sort of need I felt. My life would be completely purposeless without my daughter.

'Well,' says Nell, when I finish telling her about Megan, 'have you decided yet whether or not you'd like to meet up with your mother?'

I am a bit taken aback by Nell's bluntness, and about the word 'mother'. I am taken aback, but not upset.

I get up to fetch the letter, because I know Nell is dying to see it.

She reads it and remarks on the use of a fountain pen, but I can see that she's having as much trouble as I did in getting a picture of the author.

'She's not giving much away, is she?'

Nell shakes her head. 'I expect she feels like you do. It's a big step for both of you, which is probably why you're both being so cautious.' She looks up from the letter, smiles, 'But she does sound pleased that you've made contact.'

I give Nell a meaningful look, a reminder

that it wasn't *me* who actually made the contact. 'Perhaps.'

'So what are you going to do?'

'I think I would like to meet her.' I sip some wine and remember how important meeting her seemed this morning. 'But not straight away. I want to get used to the idea first.' And I want to sort out how this affects my relationship with my dead parents, but I don't feel like telling Nell this.

Nell looks pleased. 'That sounds fine. You could drop a line, keep up the contact, but say you're not ready to take it any further just yet. She'll understand, I'm sure.'

I give Nell a look. A look which tells her she's at it again, trying to organise me.

She claps her hand over her mouth. 'Sorry, Anna. You must do exactly what you want to do.'

'I will, and I'll probably do just what you've suggested.'

I weary suddenly of it all. When I think of what has gone on today, it's a miracle I'm not in a state of collapse. What I need now is some more light relief, so I take the letter back from Nell, put it away in the envelope, and then tell her about Jack Bailey.

When I look at her, her jaw has actually dropped. She makes a small sound which might be the beginnings of laughter, then

98

stops, mouth clammed shut again. If I had any lingering suspicions about Nell's involvement, then this reaction has put paid to them. Nell is not that good an actress.

'Crikey!' she says at last. She uses words like *crikey* and *golly* a lot, does Nell.

I decide not to mention the bit about Jack Bailey's *reputation*, as disclosed to me by Helena Chopin. I don't want Nell getting all protective and putting me off, because now that I've made up my mind to see him, I'm actually looking forward to it. I think I like the fact that he's a bit of a womaniser, and now that I've thought about it, the very fact that he *is* so much younger than I am. It makes things so much simpler, because I'll know where I am from the start. It will be about basic things such as sex, and that I can handle. It's all the other stuff I have problems with.

'Well?' I say, quite amused by her startled expression, 'is that all you can say? I thought you'd be pleased. I thought it was what you wanted to happen.'

'Anna, I am pleased, really. But I didn't really think that it would happen.' She shakes her head. 'No, don't get me wrong. I'm not surprised that he's interested in you. I mean, you're a very attractive woman . . . it's just that he *is* a lot younger . . . Oh, blow it, Anna, the truth is that I'm green with envy!'

I've had a busy day today. The first thing I did
was get off a quick note to Josephine Brown.
I kept it as brief as her letter, as completely
lacking in detail about me and my life, and
emotion. I told her how pleased I was to hear
from her, and that I would like to meet her
some time in the future if *she* wanted to, but
not just yet, and left it at that.

I had a call from Hilary as well this
morning. I was digging up a conifer at the
time and found her gushing voice recorded
on my answerphone when I was finished. She
told me how wonderful it was seeing me
again last night, which I don't believe for a
moment; how boring the meeting was at the
village hall, which I believe most sincerely;
and how she and Raymond would love me to
come to dinner sometime, and how would
Friday suit me?

I didn't know what to make of that bit, not
at first. But it didn't take long for the penny
to drop. She still has a few months of gloating
to get out of her system, and now, with
Michael away, the perfect opportunity has
presented itself. Or she thinks that it has. She
probably believes I will jump at her invitation:
poor little Anna, who rarely goes out these
days. 'Bitch!' I yelled at the answerphone, as I

washed the muck off my hands in the kitchen sink. 'I'd rather stay in alone for the rest of my life than have dinner with you!'

A bit childish, I know, but it felt good at the time.

Later, I managed three hours of typing for Harry and didn't make nearly so many mistakes as I did yesterday. I loved his chapter on how a local farm worker got his own back on a mean and crabby employer by throttling her collection of rare capons and claiming a fox had got them. I felt a bit sorry for the capons, but if anyone deserved to suffer loss then it was that mean and crabby employer. I couldn't help wondering how much loss the ex-typist would have felt if I had managed to do away with Michael.

★　★　★

As I am recalling my fairly full day, I go through the whole ritual of dressing to meet Jack Bailey again. Same clothes, same make-up.

I think the thing I feel most satisfied about is getting rid of the M & S French Collection of chocolates and the rest of the evidence — Harry's bottle which contained the strychnine, the Rescue Remedy dropper I'd used to dispense the poison with. I couldn't think what to do with them for ages. I couldn't just dump them in some anonymous dustbin, as I'd dumped the shiny red paper and silver ribbon. A dog may have found them, or worse, a child. It was good old 'Brookside' that gave me the answer in the end. I was gazing out of the kitchen window over my garden, when I suddenly thought about that woman who killed her horrible husband and what she and her daughter did with the body, and I knew what to do. So I dug up the miniature blue conifer, placed the box in the hole, and put the tree back on top. So much for soap operas being a waste of time.

Since then, I've been trying to ignore new and inventive ways of disposing of Michael as they pop uninvited into my head. When they do pop into my head, I remind myself of the awfulness of yesterday. And besides, I say to myself, why would you want Michael dead now? When you're over the worst bit, when you're beginning to sort your life out, when you're on the verge of a sexual adventure, when all you have to do is tell him to get lost when he asks for your things?

By now my hair has lost its 'just got out of bed' look. It sounds easy. It sounds as if you can just get out of bed and leave it. But it isn't like that at all. You have to work hard at getting it right, just as I'm sure Sir Cliff Richard has to work very hard at getting the carelessly-casual look just right.

So my hair is more or less back to normal, except that I've pinned it up, because it was pinned up on the night of the ceilidh, and Nell said it suited me that way, and Jack Bailey had clearly liked it that way.

It isn't until the door bell rings that I realise how nervous I am.

He smiles at me as I open the door. A nice smile, a confident smile, but I can tell he is a little less sure of himself than he was at the ceilidh. His presence in my house is strong but not overpowering. He's tall, and broad, and he's got really nice hair, very thick, and it curls a bit where it meets his shirt collar. Michael would die for hair like his, I think, as I follow him into my sitting room.

I can't help wondering who Hilary would liken him to, which gives me an idea, and before Jack Bailey gets a chance to speak, I ask him if he's free on Friday night.

He looks surprised, and I don't blame him. I'm surprised myself. It's probably because I'm so nervous. I always blab when I'm nervous, say all sorts of things I wouldn't normally dream of saying. I can feel my face hot now with embarrassment, and I wish to God I'd kept my big mouth shut.

'For anything special?' he asks, and I tell him about these people I know who've asked me to dinner and how, if he was free, he could come along too.

'Okay,' he says, looking at my red face, 'I'd love to.'

'Good,' I reply, because despite all my surprise and embarrassment, it seems the only appropriate thing to say.

'Help yourself to a drink,' I add, pointing to the drinks tray. 'I've just got a call to make, then we can go.'

In the kitchen, I take a few deep breaths and try to think rationally about this. It's no big deal. He asked to see me in the first place so what's wrong with me asking him out? It probably just makes me sound confident, a woman who knows her own mind, a sophisticated older woman of the nineties. And he did say yes, and I wasn't exactly twisting his arm. He could have invented an excuse if he didn't want to go. So I shrug and get my address book out of my bag, look up Hilary's number — which amazingly I haven't crossed out yet — and tap it in.

She answers quickly.

'Hilary!' I gush, as she had gushed, 'thanks for the call. Sorry I didn't get back sooner, I've been so busy.'

I don't let her say much.

'I'd love to come to dinner on Friday. Would it be all right if I bring a friend along?'

'Great. Come at seven-thirty.'

'Okay. See you then. Must dash.'

Am I going mad? I wonder, as I replace the receiver. Is that why I tried to kill Michael? Then I realise that the very fact I am considering this possibility rules it out. People who are mad don't know that they are. What a relief. Only the relief is short-lived. Because then I realise that if I'm not mad, I am certainly bad, *and* sad — a pathetic middle-aged woman, desperate to show people she really does have a life, that she is capable of getting herself a man, even though the best she can get is one with a terrible reputation with women.

Jack Bailey is holding a glass of something amber-coloured in his hand and looking at the photo of Megan when I return to the sitting room.

'Pretty girl,' he says. 'Is she a relative? She looks a bit like you.'

A bit, but not much. On the whole, since Michael has more physical good points than I have, Megan is more like her father. But, thank God, she does have my lips. 'My daughter,' I tell him, hoping my voice sounds steadier to him than it does to me. I can tell he thinks he should say something corny like, 'you don't look old enough to have a daughter that age', but I'm glad that he doesn't.

Suddenly I cannot bear to go out. I think it's because I'm reminded that Megan is closer to Jack Bailey's age than to mine and the thought of being seen with him has made me even more uncomfortable. I couldn't handle it in my present state. The feeling's so strong that I couldn't care less about *sexual adventures* right now and would send Jack Bailey packing if I could think of a way of doing it without being rude again. So I decide on a compromise.

'It's just occurred to me,' I say with such forced brightness I get a pain in my jaw, 'why go out? We've got all the drinks we need here and we don't have to worry about driving then.'

He shrugs and smiles. A smile that makes his eyes crinkle at the corners. Brown eyes, I notice, very nice brown eyes. But what does that smile mean? Has he taken my suggestion as some sort of sexual invitation? Is it a sexual invitation?

'Suits me,' he says. 'It's a great evening, maybe we could sit in the garden for a while.'

I relax a bit on hearing this. He can't be expecting me to get up to anything in the garden, so at least he's prepared to pace this a little, get to know me a bit before we get down to business. I find myself warming to him. He's good at this, I think, good at making his would-be conquest feel at her ease. And I like the way he is dressed: jeans, tee-shirt, with an unbuttoned checked shirt on top. And I feel, I don't know what I feel. Confused, mostly.

I top up his drink, which is whisky and dry, and make the same for myself.

'I know this house quite well,' Jack Bailey tells me. 'I did some work on it for the people you bought it from. The Proctors. Nice couple.'

I ask him which particular bit of work he did on the house and he tells me the bathroom and some odd bits in the kitchen.

'Oh, yes, and I put the fitted wardrobes in the main bedroom. Very tasteful, I thought.'

I wonder why we are talking this way. Maybe I've got it all wrong. Maybe he's just here to tout for more business.

In the garden, we sit on ornate green Victorian-style metal seats which I bought from Do It All a week after I moved in. Not bad for the price, though this is the first time I've had any use for them.

I can't think of anything to say to him. I'm suddenly horribly conscious of the fact that I must look really old in natural light. It's made me edgy again, so that I find it difficult to look at him, never mind speak to him. I'm probably making him feel uncomfortable, because he obviously can't think of anything to say to me either.

I force my features into what I hope is a soft, contemplative smile, and try to look as if I am softly contemplating the garden. Which is really quite pretty, despite the fact that there isn't much out yet and I haven't had the time, or rather the inclination, to plant any annuals. Still, there's plenty of greenery, with lost of creeping things I don't know the name of growing over the walls.

I find that my eyes keep drifting towards the blue conifer and when I feel Jack Bailey looking at me, I am forced to say something, anything.

'I'm a terrible gardener,' I tell him, because it's the first thing which comes into my head, and because it's the truth. 'I've always had this idea that I'd become an expert one day, but so far I haven't even got as far as a library book on the subject.'

'I know what you mean. I've always wanted to be a champion water skier, but I haven't even learned to swim yet.'

I find myself laughing. 'Are you serious?' I am disarmed by this admission. I thought everyone could swim.

'Absolutely,' he says with a grin. 'I missed out when I was a kid. It just wasn't on the family agenda, and I was at one of those schools where sport of any kind was very low down on the priority list.'

So then I ask him about his family, and find out that he has two older sisters, who live in the south; that his parents, who he sees quite a lot, live not all that far away, in Keighley. It turns out that his father works in a factory, and for some reason I am pleased to hear this.

'So we do have something in common,' I say. 'My father worked in a factory too, though I haven't a clue what sort of factory. He was a man of few words, I'm afraid.'

'So's mine, which makes two things we have in common.'

I return his smile, get up and fetch more drinks, and crisps in a bowl, and as we compare notes on our taciturn, working-class fathers, I find myself beginning to relax. Really relax.

'So what was your mother like?' he asks, when we've exhausted fathers.

'She always had an encouraging word about potato crops,' I tell him, and then I explain about my father's passion in life, and without meaning to, about never really feeling part of the closeness the two of them shared.

Which was only a small step from telling him about being adopted and about my discovery when I was eight.

However, since this isn't the sort of thing I usually pour out to someone I've only met once before, and since it most certainly isn't the sort of thing you're supposed to pour out to someone with sexual conquest on their mind, I regret such pourings-out immediately.

I suspect he is very embarrassed, and I should like to disappear in the proverbial puff of smoke. Right now, I wish that life really was like a soap opera. That we could cut the scene here and start filming again when he's gone: *Anna alone in her kitchen — washing two glasses, frowning, shaking her head a little, showing, through subtle facial expressions, her regrets about not keeping the conversation light-hearted and simple.*

'I have a cousin who was adopted,' he says after an age. 'I've talked to her about it a couple of times and I think she feels like you do. She had a happy enough childhood but she never felt as if she really *belonged*.' I can sense him looking at me, and I just hope I don't make this worse by starting to snivel, and the only way I can be sure I won't is to change the subject. So I say the first thing which comes into my head. Which I have found is very often a big mistake.

'So how old *are* you?' I ask him, and then feel like biting my tongue off.

He is smiling again, not at all fazed by the bluntness and suddenness of my question.

'How old would you like me to be?'

I think the whisky must be taking effect. I find myself smiling as well. I try to think of an acceptable age difference. 'Thirty-eight would be good.'

'Thirty-eight it is then.'

He's grinning again now, and I'm hopeful that, by accident almost, the situation has been retrieved. I'm even wondering what it would be like to be kissed by him, which means I have probably had quite enough to drink. I advise myself to have no more.

'Are you ready for another?' I ask him, never being one to take good advice when it's offered.

'If we can drink it inside,' he says. 'It's getting a bit cool out here.'

He's right, it is. I hadn't noticed till now, but I'm actually shivering a little.

So we get up and go inside and as I pour more whisky, I am aware that he is standing behind me. He should be sitting down by now, but he's not, and I am very conscious of his closeness.

'Anna?'

Oh God, he sounds strange. Is this it, the beginning. Bloody hell, what do I do? I've never actually had a sexual adventure before. I turn and he takes the drinks I am holding and puts them down.

'Now that we've sorted out the age thing . . . ' he begins, then stops again.

I notice that his breathing is a bit odd. He is standing so close that I can smell his whisky-and-dry breath and I expect he can smell mine. I feel peculiar. I can feel pulses pounding in unfamiliar places. My head feels light. I feel a bit sick.

Please don't let me be sick.

He puts his hands on my shoulders, and it occurs to me that he might be about to strangle me, and all the symptoms I'm having now are fear.

Fight or flight.

Only then he pulls me to him, and I can feel him trembling, like he's afraid, too.

Now his hands are in my hair. He's removing the pins which are holding it up, and I realise I am not about to die after all.

I am being seduced.

I am being seduced by a young man with a *reputation*

And I'm not resisting.

And then my mind cuts out and my body takes over — or it almost does. I do know a moment's panic when I can't remember what underwear I've got on, that I should probably have shaved my legs. But I am clearly not so panicked that it prevents me taking his hand and leading him towards the staircase.

Despite all my present uncertainties, uppermost in my mind at this moment is the knowledge that sex, at my age, is more comfortable in bed than it is on the sitting-room floor.

Erotic Promises and
Teddy Bears

Today, I cannot imagine why I ever wanted to kill Michael. How he could ever have been that important.

I really must have been mad for a while, in the throes of some sort of breakdown, as a result perhaps of all the things which have happened over the past few months.

And, if it was the letter from Josephine Brown which arrested the madness, then it is sex which has cured it. I was right about Jack, I was right to choose someone with whom I knew exactly what to expect. It puts an immediate block on all those girlish notions about love and happy-ever-afterness. In fact, this morning, I feel more like one of those wicked older women who kept on seducing poor Tom Jones as he pursued the lovely Sophia Western over half the country. Not as if Tom Jones was exactly an innocent, any more than Jack is.

It was amazing, and I had no idea that I had so much stamina. Apart from half an hour or so of rest every now and then, we must have been at it for about seven hours in all. And one of the best bits didn't happen till he was leaving. It was then that we made a promise. We would not, we agreed, have sex the same way twice until we had completely run out of new ideas.

It is the most excitingly erotic promise I have ever made anyone. It is the only erotic promise I have ever made anyone, come to think of it.

He is coming around tonight, as soon as he finishes work, and I cannot wait to start keeping that promise. I have been thinking of *new ways* ever since he left this morning. I thought about going to the library, or a bookshop, perhaps even buying a video, but I think I have enough ideas of my own to be going on with. And I expect Jack will have plenty of ideas as well.

He left at seven, and I couldn't have cared less what the neighbours thought about his white van being parked outside my house all night.

I got up straight away and moved a pair of tall candelabra from my junk room into my lemon and pale green bedroom. Five foot high, they are, with fat churchy candles that will last all night. I felt like a film director, setting a major, pivotal scene in a thought-provoking, low-budget, erotic movie, one that will probably do surprisingly well at the box office, gain a cult following in the States, make its stars and director famous.

Then I got into the bath and while I shaved my legs in the luxury of essence of rosemary and lavender, I planned a shopping trip for new underwear and relived the whole night again in my mind. Then I thought about Paul, and how even my fantasies about him paled in the reality of Jack. I met Paul four years ago. On an Antiques Appreciation course. He was the tutor. He was tall and thin and had a slightly tortured appearance; he was exactly as I would have expected a romantic poet to look.

Nothing happened between us, but I know I would have liked something to happen. We wrote to each other for a while. We wrote about antiques and our latest finds and bargains. There was nothing intimate or personal about the letters he wrote to me but I let my mind have full rein on its fantasies, and I pretended that between those prosaic lines was the same deep passion that I felt for him. I kept all of his letters and when, one day, I was particularly needy, I steamed off one of the stamps on an envelope and licked it, knowing that he had licked it before me. It was the closest I ever felt or got to him.

It wasn't long after that when he stopped

writing to me. I was distraught. That fantasy had kept me going for ages, made my marriage to Michael seem almost bearable. After that it felt worse, much worse. Which just goes to show what a mistake all that love and passion stuff is.

The phone rang while I was in the bath. I think it must have been Nell but she didn't leave a message. I know she will be dying to hear how things went with Jack but I'm not sure I'm-ready to tell her just yet.

I rather regret having to go and type for Harry today, but I can't let him down. So I dress with more care than usual and tell myself that the evening will be here before I know it.

★ ★ ★

On the way to Harry's, I turn off into the lane which leads to my old house. I have decided to drop the bird prints off. If I don't do it now Michael will only ring me when he gets back and I can do without that. I shouldn't let him have them, I know, but that really is it. No more. Not ever.

Despite everything that has happened over the last couple of days, all the things I have realised, I can't help feeling resentful when I look at my old home. I lived in this house for ten years and put a lot of work into making it the beautiful home it is today.

The view from my old home is wonderful. Especially now, with the soft-hued greenness of early summer. The house, which is old but not so old as the house I now live in, is on the edge of a gorge. I *think* it can be described as a gorge, it is certainly too steep to be called a valley or dale. If it were not for the limestone beneath the house, it may well have slipped its foundations by now, so close is it to the edge of the gorge.

From the side of the house, a path winds steeply down to a fast-running stream, which is hidden from here by a wood. I know that if I walk down into the wood I will see the bluishgrey haze of dying bluebells and, just as the ground levels out next to the stream, I will come upon my favourite beech tree. It is the most perfect specimen of its kind I have ever seen, with sprawling, reaching branches that form a sheltering, leafy bower.

Often, when I returned from walking the dogs, I would sit with my back against the tree's sturdy trunk, and while the dogs sniffed about in the wood, I would dream. I always felt safe there and sometimes, when I was being particularly fanciful, I would wonder if it was possible to fall in love with a tree. It was the closest I ever came to being

118

unfaithful to Michael (except for Paul, but I don't think he counts, either).

I decide to leave the prints in the garage which is always open, because the lock is broken, and prop the prints against Shelly's new car: a nice little black convertible, which I've heard was a gift from Michael. And to think how long it took before I got my own car, and how long we did without fancy holidays in the likes of the Florida Quays. I consider jumping on the exhaust but resist the temptation. Petty vandalism, I decide, just isn't my style.

Then I close the door and go back to the front of the house, and I find myself staring at the door.

Michael is far too careless about his home. Just because it has never been burgled is no good reason to assume that it never will be. He really should install an alarm system. But he's too mean for that. Which is very foolish of him.

I find I am smiling. I don't know why, but I am suddenly overcome by an odd feeling of tenderness towards my mean and foolish ex-husband. I feel like doing him a service. I feel like showing him what a mistake it is not to protect his home. I mean, if I find no difficulty in breaking in, think how easy it would be for a professional.

It couldn't be easier.

Nip round the back, picking a likely looking rock from the dry-stone wall on the way. Take off my jumper, wrap it round the stone, to dull the sound (not that there's anyone around to hear, but better be on the safe side) . . . swing it against the dining-room window . . . wait while the glass settles . . . move dangerous looking pieces out of the way with the jumper covering my hand, so as not to leave any fingerprints . . . keep my hand covered as I put it through the jagged gap in the window . . . turn the latch . . . open the window . . . heave myself up. And I am inside.

Simple as that.

The house sounds strangely silent, and it smells different from the way it smelt when I lived here. Not really unpleasant, just different.

I notice that the dining-room fireplace has some white antique lace draped over it. It looks wrong; it isn't that kind of fireplace. But there have been few other changes. There are some gaps where the things I took used to be, but mostly they have been filled with similar items, or with things Michael has gradually wheedled back from me.

I go into the kitchen, tiptoeing about as if I am afraid of disturbing someone. No change here, either, except for some new plants. A big spider plant on the windowsill, one I don't have a name for on the table. My glass rolling pins are badly displayed, and the copper pots, Delftware and Worcester are nowhere to be seen. If he didn't want them on show, why did he want them at all? I stand back and take it all in. All very neat and tidy — not even a bowl of withering fruit to be seen — much tidier than when I lived here.

The main sitting room has some new curtains and a sofa: not very nice — a bit tacky — which I find very pleasing. I am pleased that the ex-typist has such bad taste.

Not so pleasing, is the fact that my grandfather clock is not in the place that it used to be. It stands now in a corner, and it looks all wrong there. It *is* all wrong there. And it's not even ticking. They didn't even bother to wind it up before they went away.

I take in my other possessions. It makes me mad to see them here. It makes me realise what a fool I have been.

I go upstairs, not tiptoeing anymore, and I am shocked when I go into my old bedroom. The same ornate iron bed stands in the same position, but piled on a new white lace counterpane are dozens of teddy bears. If I hadn't known better I would have thought I'd wandered into the room of a child. I don't know whether to laugh at this or be mad. I suppose it is funny to think of Michael having to take all those teddies off the bed before he can get into it. Or maybe she does that. Then my mind wanders a bit and I try to imagine the two of them here in this bed, the same bed I shared with Michael for years, and God, that does make me mad. How could he share with her the same bed he shared with me? And how could *she* bring herself to sleep, have sex, in the same bed he slept and had sex in with me?

And now, without thinking about it very hard first, I nip back down to the kitchen and open the freezer section of the fridge. I pull bags out to see what's in them, then shove them all back again when I find what I didn't even know I was looking for. I spend a while searching for some kind of sewing box, but have to make do with one of those freebie kits found in hotel bedrooms. The only scissors I can find are some nail ones which I come across in a bathroom cabinet.

Back in my old bedroom, I sit on the prissy, white lace counterpane and choose three teddy bears at random. I don't feel a bit sorry as I plunge the scissors in the back seam of each of them and make a slit. Then I pull out some of their stuffing, stick that into my jacket pocket, and replace the filling with frozen mincemeat.

It will be a while before it gets nice and high, I think, as I sew each of the teddy bears carefully back up.

I feel very satisfied about this. Even though I know it's petty and silly and not at all grown up, I reckon that after all Michael has put me through he deserves just a little bit of comeback. Perhaps even more than a bit.

It occurs to me when I'm putting what's left of the meat back in the freezer — an idea that might well be deemed 'more than a bit' of comeback. I hesitate, think about 'letting go' and 'moving on', and all the sensible advice I've been giving myself over the past couple of days, and yet I still put the plug in the sink and turn on the cold tap.

I admit I am glowing, as Nell glows, when I climb back out of the window. I feel great, pleased with life. My only regret is that I didn't do something like this ages ago; if I had, then maybe I wouldn't have ended up wanting to kill my ex-husband.

★　★　★

I didn't stay long with Harry today. He'd done a bit of typing himself and I estimate that at least half the book has now been processed. He seemed pleased about this when I told him, but not as pleased as I thought he would be. He said I had an extra sparkle about me today but I didn't tell him the cause of the sparkle, or the possible cause.

He asked me to stay and share a glass of sloe gin with him, but I kept thinking of Jack and the things we would be doing later, and I made my excuses. I told him I probably wouldn't be able to make it tomorrow but, if he liked, I could come over on Saturday. It wasn't until I was getting into my car that I realised how quiet Harry had been.

★　★　★

The Davidsons live in a smart new house on a tree-lined hill just outside Ilkley centre: the most expensive part of the town. Raymond makes his money by selling health insurance, and since he seems to make rather a lot of money, I have to assume that he is very good at his job.

Hilary is a typical Ilkley housewife. Lots of entertaining and lunching and charity events. She once worked as a receptionist at the same firm as Raymond, but I think she prefers to forget about that period in her life.

Their home is all onyx and festoon blinds and big, imported china animals that sit disconcertingly about the house. I think that they have them instead of pets, which would be far too messy for someone like Hilary. I suspect it is for similar reasons that their three children have been sent away to expensive schools, but I may be misjudging the Davidsons about this.

They have a built-in bar in the corner of their sitting room, with real beer pumps, and optics for spirits. And to the sound of Barry Manilow performing his seventies and eighties hits, Raymond is now pouring drinks from behind his bar. He has some sort of serving cloth over his shoulder, just like a real cocktail barman.

'I can't get over how well Anna looks,' Hilary is saying to Raymond, as he pulls a half pint of beer for Jack. I think he is disappointed that I only want wine: his stainless steel cocktail shaker looks ready for business.

Hilary sounds genuinely astounded at my apparent good health and she is looking at Jack now with undisguised curiosity. She is trying to work out what he is to me, and wondering how she may politely find out without sounding too obvious. She is an open book.

'I think you've lost some weight, haven't you, Anna?'

'Not that I'm aware of,' I reply.

Jack brushes his arm against mine as he reaches to take his drink from Raymond, and I wish I was at home in bed with him. I wonder if I can bear not to touch him for however long we will have to be here. I found out on the way here that he is going away on Sunday for five days. He is doing some sort of building job in a distant dale, too far to return at night. He wouldn't normally work so far away, he told me, but he needs the money. If I'd known before that he was going away, I would never have come here.

We sit down together on the sofa, and put our drinks on the onyx coffee table.

Hilary is a determinedly cheerful hostess and is rarely lost for a conversation piece, but she seems to be struggling now. She sits in a deep cream-coloured, damask armchair and shows us most of her short legs as she crosses them.

'Do come and sit down, Raymond', she says, smiling grimly at her husband, clearly in need of support. 'I hope you like lamb, um . . . Jack. I forgot to ask Anna if her guest was a vegetarian — there are so many about these days,' she adds, making vegetarianism sound like a dose of flu.

'Lamb's fine by me,' Jack replies, charmingly.

'What is it you do, Jack?' Hilary wants to know.

He tells her that he is a builder, which startles her somewhat. She looks uncertain whether her social lexicon will be able to cope with this. But it clearly intrigues her all the more — it's all there in her face.

Raymond joins us now, and Hilary relaxes a little. She seems to be flirting a little with Jack, playing with her shortish hair sort of sexily, putting on a bit of a Texan accent.

On the wall behind her is a rather large portrait of Hilary, an extremely flattering portrait, so flattering it does actually make her look a bit like Jerry Hall. I comment on it and she bats her eyelids. 'I had it done for Raymond's last birthday,' she says, turning round to admire her flattering image. 'He was thrilled, weren't you, Raymond?'

Raymond, I have to say, doesn't look all that thrilled at the moment. He seems rather embarrassed, in fact.

As usual, he has little to say. Although he does make an effort, once he's established that Jack isn't interested in private health insurance, or golf, he gets down to some serious drinking, which, I recall, he has always preferred to conversation. He seems content to let Hilary do the talking.

As I look at the two of them, sitting in their

separate armchairs, I am struck for the first time by an almost tangible gulf between them. They remind me of myself and Michael when we were together. Perhaps I have been gifted with sudden new insight into human relationships, because for years I thought that this marriage worked; but then for years I thought my own marriage worked — of course, I'd just been kidding myself. Then I realise why I felt strangely cheered following Hilary's recent visit to my home. I look at her again, then at Raymond, think of other nights when I have been here with Michael. It was the simple pleasure of knowing I am no longer a part of all this.

'Your house is remarkable,' Jack says suddenly.

Can he possibly be serious?

Hilary looks thrilled. 'Oh Jack, do you really think so?' She jumps up from her seat. 'Would you like me to give you a guided tour? We've just had the place redecorated.' She glances at me. 'We had an interior designer in. Very expensive, but I think it was worth it.'

I'd ask for my money back, I'm thinking. I hadn't even noticed that there had been any changes.

Hilary drags Jack off, and since I don't seem to be included in the invitation, this leaves me alone with Raymond.

'How's the handicap going?' I say, because experience tells me I will be safe with golf.

'No change,' he replies. He gets up and pours himself another large gin. 'I've been stuck at sixteen for three and a half years and I can't see it improving now.' He sounds fed up, and I have a feeling there is more to it than a static golf handicap.

'More wine?'

'No thanks, Raymond, but I wouldn't mind trying a cocktail.'

He looks pleased.

'Shall I surprise you?'

'Go on then.'

I join him at the bar as he adds Lord knows what to the stainless steel cocktail shaker. He is in his element, and I'm glad to have provided him with a sense of purpose.

He pours something blue into a glass and passes it to me.

'I created that one myself,' he says. 'I call it *Ray's Blue Heaven*.'

I try not to laugh.

'Cheers Raymond.' I take a sip. 'Mmm, that's good.' It was okay.

He seems ludicrously pleased with himself and I suddenly feel very sorry for him.

He looks at me over the bar and I have the feeling he is seeing me properly for the first time since I arrived.

'So there is life after marriage, then, Anna?'

I can tell it's no idle enquiry, and I'm not sure how to respond to this. I am saved from trying by the sound of Hilary's coquettish laughter as she and Jack come back into the room.

We eat melon and the lamb and then Lemon Something-or-other — all fairly indifferent — while Hilary flirts shamelessly with Jack. Having assured her that her taste was *matchless*, following his guided tour, she has decided to overlook his questionable social standing and is now clearly finding him fascinating.

By the time three bottles of wine are consumed, mainly by Hilary and Raymond, Hilary eventually feels reckless enough for bluntness. She looks at Jack and then at me.

'So, come on, you two. Are you two just friends, or is there more to it than that?' The *Texan* drawl is quite strong now, I note, and when I glance briefly at Raymond I can see his discomfort.

But I am feeling rather reckless too. So I look at Jack, see a definite twinkle in his eye, then smile what I hope is a secretive sort of smile.

'There's more to it than that,' I reply.

Hilary plants her elbows on the table, stares at me.

I nudge Jack with my knee under the table, as a warning, then I relax back into my chair.

'Well?' prompts Hilary.

'It's about sex,' I say quietly, because the room is so silent I could get away with a whisper. I glance at Raymond again and see he's not looking uncomfortable now. His elbows are on the table as well. He is all ears.

'Well!' Hilary says again, only this time it comes out as an exclamation.

'Well, well, well,' says Raymond.

Then Jack reaches over and takes my hand, grins at me, 'Which reminds me, Anna, don't you think it's time we were on our way?'

Varicose Veins and Frightening Telephone Calls

After a day spent in bed, we get up at six for something to eat. I have not answered the phone all day. It rang three or four times and on the last two occasions Nell left messages asking me to ring her back. She's been away at some aerobic marathon thing in Sheffield for the last couple of days, so I haven't spoken to her since that first night with Jack. By now she will be dying to know how things are going, but she'll just have to wait a bit longer.

We laughed a lot on the way home from the Davidsons' last night. Especially about Hilary's look-alike obsession, and her insistence that Jack was the living image of Keanu Reeves. 'Though not quite as exotic, of course.' And when he told me she looked more like Lily Savage than Jerry Hall, and had interior design taste to match her looks, my cup runneth over.

As we sit at my kitchen table munching cheese and crackers and wrinkly apples, Jack is wearing one of my old baggy jumpers with his jeans and I, for some reason, am wearing my best, rarely worn, cotton dressing-gown. I don't go in much for glamour nightwear and this is the closest thing I have to anything which might be described as remotely sexy. I feel uncomfortable wearing it. It's flimsy and see-through, and it shows off too many imperfections.

I worried a lot about my varicose veins at first, the very worst of my many imperfections. I am sure Jack will never have seen anything quite so horrible and ugly before. I tried hiding them from him, as I hid them from Michael, but that's not so easy with someone like Jack. Someone who seems interested in practically every part of a woman's body. And although I squirmed as he ran his fingers over those hideous blemishes, it was quite a relief, I suppose, that he did at least know the score. It was a bit confusing though, because at the time it didn't seem to have very much to do with sex.

'Tell me about your life with Michael,' Jack is saying to me now. It's chilly today, chilly for June. There's been some rain and to make things cosy I've lit a couple of candles and got Jack to move the table a bit closer to the Rayburn.

Life with Michael? Did I have a life with

Michael? I'm not sure that I did. My life just sort of tagged on to his life. But Jack doesn't want to hear that. I'm surprised he's even asked the question.

'It was great,' I say. 'For the first couple of weeks. It was just the last twenty-two years that weren't so brilliant.'

Jack is half-frowning, half-smiling at me. He can't work out whether I am being serious or not. He thinks I am exaggerating. I am. The fact is, it was going wrong even before we married. Sometimes I wonder if it was ever right. Sometimes I think I only married Michael because he asked me and because he was so certain I would accept. But since only an idiot would marry someone on that sort of basis, I shall not be admitting to it.

'If it was that bad, why did you stay?'

'Because I got pregnant with Megan very quickly.'

'So was he always unfaithful?' I have told him the gist of what happened seven and a half months ago.

I swallow a piece of tasteless cheddar with difficulty. 'Probably.' Odd, but I've never allowed myself to admit this before. I'm sure that if anyone had asked me this even a week ago, I would have denied it.

Jack isn't half-smiling now.

'I know what you're thinking. You're

wondering how any self-respecting woman put up with a philanderer for twenty-odd years. Well, like I say, there was Megan, and then there was the little question of proof — if he *was* philandering, then he was fairly discreet about it, I'll give him that at least. But mostly it was because, bit by bit, he somehow managed to make me believe that I couldn't function without him.'

How clear it all seems suddenly, when I have been struggling for years for explanations. How much sense I seem to make when I'm talking to a man with whom there is no emotional involvement.

Jack begins peeling a wrinkly apple.

'So why did you leave in the end?'

'Because Megan was gone and I finally did have proof.'

He cuts the apple in two halves and passes one half to me. 'And you found that you *could* function without him after all.'

I look at him over the table. If he knew what I'd been up to over the last couple of weeks he may have had his doubts about this. I begin to feel uneasy. If I'm not very careful I'll end up telling him everything, and, well, I can't do that. So I get up from the table, my half of the apple untouched.

'I've got something to show you,' I say, opening the kitchen drawer. I take out the

Millet engraving and pass it to him. 'What do you think?' I ask. 'Any idea what it means?'

He frowns at the strange goings on in the picture. Then he shakes his head. 'No idea, I'm afraid. Some mythical tale, perhaps: Greek, Roman, I'm not sure.'

I take it back from him and feel Jack's eyes on me as I study it again. The wood in the background seems suddenly more sinister than it did before, and the light on the path where the woman is being led, seems brighter. I'm sure that must mean something but I cannot think what.

'Is there anything special about it?' Jack asks. 'I mean, why all the interest in some old print?'

'Engraving,' I correct him. 'Don't know, really. I just hate not understanding something.' I get up and put the engraving away, make another mental note to get it reframed.

When I sit down again, Jack takes my hands over the table and I'm glad of the dim light as he examines my fingernails. It's not my nails which bother me but my wrinkly hands, which are almost as bad as the apples. I have never bothered with rubber gloves or lashings of hand cream, and wear and tear has taken its grisly toll.

But he does not seem to notice.

'Tell me some more about yourself,' he

says. 'Your childhood, what you were like as a teenager, what you did before you met Michael?'

So I give him an edited, slightly glamorised version of my life up until Michael, to make it more interesting. Then he brings up the adoption thing again, and because he seems genuinely interested, I tell him about Josephine Brown and the letter I had from her this very week.

'You should meet her,' he says. 'There's a lot she can tell you about yourself. I've never much gone for the *Nurture* argument, I'm convinced our genes are a lot more important than our environment.'

I think about this, recall a similar conversation with Nell. 'That's okay if Josephine Brown turns out to be what I'd like her to be, but what if she's awful? What's that going to do for my sense of who I am?'

'I doubt that very much,' he says, then squeezes my hand and looks into my face. 'My bet is that she'll be very special.'

We drink some wine and I make Jack tell me more about his life. About a reasonably happy childhood in Keighley, his time at Leeds University — which was a reasonably happy experience, as well; how he eventually got into the building trade, which he prefers far more than anything a history degree prepared him for. The only thing he does not tell me about are the women before me, and I don't ask about them.

Then we go back to bed and this time we sleep. We sleep until early morning and then begin our lovemaking all over again. Or rather, we begin to have sex all over again.

★ ★ ★

I am tired when he leaves and a bit sad as well. The tiredness is understandable but I tell myself off for the sad bit, remind myself what my relationship with Jack is about and refuse to entertain any gooey feelings, just because he has been nice to me.

There have been a few other calls from Nell, so, at midday I decide I cannot put off ringing her back any longer.

She is a while answering the phone and I try to compose myself as I listen to the ringing tone, knowing that she will want to know all about Jack. How am I going to handle this? Coolly? Matter-of-factly? Woman-of-the-wordly?

'Anna!' she sighs 'Thank God. I was beginning to worry about you. I take it you haven't heard about Harry? I was going to leave a message on the answerphone but I didn't want to frighten you.'

'What about Harry?' I feel a dragging

sensation in my stomach.

'He's in hospital, Anna. He was taken in yesterday. Luckily someone went round to see him and they called an ambulance straight away.'

I feel terrible. I should have gone round yesterday. I should have been the one to see that he was ill and call the ambulance. But I was so wrapped up in myself and sex that I hardly gave Harry a thought.

I think about those chocolates. Oh God.

But no, of course it wasn't the chocolates. Strychnine acts a lot faster than that, that much I do know.

'Are you still there, Anna?'

'Is it serious?'

'I don't know yet. But he is eighty-two; I suppose most things are serious at that age.

'Where is he?'

'Airedale, Ward Three, only I don't think there's any point rushing off there now, he isn't allowed any visitors yet.'

'Okay,' I say, 'I'll ring then.'

'Where have you been, anyway, Anna? With Jack?'

I am so ashamed of myself that I would like to lie, tell her I've been away somewhere important, doing charity work or something, but I just make some affirmative grunt.

'Well, are you going to tell me about it, or

is this not the right time?' There is no disapproval in her tone but I still hate myself.

'Not the right time,' I tell her. 'I'll ring you later.'

I put the phone down and then call the hospital. There have clearly been lots of calls about Harry and when I tell the ward sister I am just a friend, and not a relative, she is a little dismissive. She tells me he is *comfortable* and that I should ring again in the morning, after the consultant has done his rounds.

★ ★ ★

I am very tired this morning and my spirits are low. I lay awake most of the night feeling guilty. About Harry. About not being there when he needed me. The guilt is so strong that it feels like a punishment for the bad things I've done.

I rang the hospital again a while ago and was told there would be tests carried out today: they weren't giving much away. So I rang Harry's sister, the only relative I know who's still living, and she told me it's something to do with his heart again.

I'm still not allowed to visit him. It's *Relatives Only* at present, which I'm glad about really, and I feel more guilt for being glad. Trouble with me is that I'm very scared of illness, and I think that has something to do with the medical dictionary I read with such fascinated horror when I was young. I have often wished that my mother had bought a different book with her penny at that school jumble sale.

★ ★ ★

The phone rings and it's Michael. Bugger him, I think, just back from a fancy holiday with that stupid little tart who has draped my dining-room fireplace with a ridiculous piece of antique lace. God, I am so angry with him that just for a moment I wish he had eaten those bloody *truffe de Calvados*.

He sounds a bit strange and I am hoping that maybe he has just been told some terrible news, that he's learnt he has only a few weeks to live.

'Can I come over and see you?' he is saying.

'I dropped the prints off in your garage, if that's what you're worried about.'

'Yes, I know, I found them. I don't suppose you saw anything odd when you were here?'

'Odd?'

'Someone broke a window in the dining room while we were away.'

Why does it still annoy me when he says *we*?

'Anything taken?' I ask, because that, I reason, would be the normal response to such a statement.

'No, thank goodness. They must have been frightened away, or maybe it was just kids messing about. But they've made a terrible mess. The ground floor has been flooded out. The carpets are ruined. Someone put the plug in the sink and left the tap on.'

As if I gave a damn about his problems. But I do see some potential for mischief, something which didn't occur to me when I put that plug in the sink. 'Maybe Shelly did it, left the tap running — accidentally, I mean. Things like that happen.' Especially to airheads. Only I keep this bit to myself.

He's quiet for a bit, then, 'I must say, that possibility had occurred to me. Still, the insurance will take care of it. Though I'm not sure what we can do about an awful smell in our bedroom. It's like something's died in there.'

I make no reply, but I find I am smiling.

'When can I come round, then?'

'Whenever. I'm not going out this evening.' Why am I saying this? I wonder. I promised myself I wouldn't let him into my house again, and now look at me.

'See you later then. About six.'

'Fine.'

Only it isn't fine. It bloody well isn't fine at all.

*   *   *

I ring Nell at five and find out from her that Harry is having surgery in the morning. Still no visitors allowed. God, it really must be serious. I tell her just a bit about Jack, about taking him to dinner at Hilary's (which she already knew about, because Hilary had rung her), and how Hilary thought he was the image of Keanu Reeves. This is supposed to lighten the mood, but it doesn't. Nell is nearly as fond of Harry as I am.

*   *   *

Michael arrives early and although I couldn't care less what he looks like, I can't really help noticing that he seems drawn. Not at all like someone who has just come back from holiday, rather like someone who really has just received some terrible news.

'You've heard about Harry, I suppose,' I say, thinking maybe it's that, although this doesn't really seem very likely because although Michael is fond of Harry, he didn't look this bad when his own grandfather died.

'Yes, poor old chap. Let's just hope he pulls through.'

I soften just a little bit towards him for that. It sounded genuine enough.

I let him into the kitchen and ask if he wants a drink, remembering the last drink I gave him. But he's safe today. Even if I still wanted to kill him I wouldn't have the heart for it with Harry so ill.

'Okay, yes please. Anything, I don't mind.'

Polite, as well. How different he is from the last time I saw him.

I go into the sitting room and pour him a whisky, because I know how much he hates it.

He looks at the glass but doesn't seem very bothered about what's in it, which is disappointing.

'Well,' I say, when it begins to seem as if he might sit there looking at the glass all night. 'Have you got something to say? Something to ask me for?'

He looks at me as if I have administered a physical blow: I see surprise, then pain — or a very competent impression of pain.

'I had a call from Hilary today,' he says.

I feel my face colour. The cow. Couldn't wait to tell him.

'And?'

'She told me about Friday and about some

builder chap you had in tow. A very young builder called Bill, or something like that.' There is emphasis on the words *young* and *builder*.

'Jack, actually,' I correct him.

'She tells me you and he are . . . well, the words that she used were 'sexually involved'.' He says this in the same way he might if he'd heard I'd just taken up fire-eating as a hobby, only I don't see quite the same incredulity in his expression.

I can't help laughing at Hilary's coy choice of words, which Michael seems to find very provoking. I can tell this by the way his eyes narrow.

He puts his thin lips to the glass and takes a swig. Only now does he realise it's whisky, apparently.

'Hell, Anna, you know I hate this bloody stuff.'

'I'd forgotten,' I say.

He puts down the offending glass, stand up, and faces me as if he is about to say something very important.

Then he pulls back and looks at the Rayburn.

'Why are you set on making such a fool of yourself, Anna?'

'I didn't realise I was. Are you telling me it is foolish to be sleeping with someone so

145

young, or someone who is a builder?'

His blue eyes flash at me. He is finding it hard to control his anger now.

'Both! Can't you imagine what people will say? Well-off, middle-aged woman and hard-up, youthful builder. It's like something you read in the tacky Sundays.'

I try to remember if there is any strychnine left. It helps keep me calm.

'Any worse than, *Well-off, middle-aged, baldy, and twenty-two-year-old ex-typist?*'

'Don't be stupid, Anna. There's no comparison. You realise he's after your money, of course.'

'So that's what's bothering you, is it? You're just worried Jack might get his hands on *your* money. Only it isn't your money Michael, it's mine. And if I choose to squander it on a gorgeous young man, then I bloody well will.'

I sound quite calm, and calmly I walk to the kitchen door and open it.

'Fuck off, Michael,' I say, in a voice so controlled I am proud of myself.

★　★　★

Harry came through the operation okay. He's had some work done on a valve or something and if he makes it over the next few days, he has a very good chance of making a full recovery. That is the official line, anyway.

I slept better last night. Jack phoned and said he was missing me, and I told him about Harry and said I was missing him too. The sex, anyway, I said to myself, to keep me from getting soppy and from thinking about what Michael had said about Jack being after my money.

I got up early and bought lots of food, and a gift and a card for Harry. I thought if I bought these things then he had to survive. This may be superstitious nonsense but it helped at the time. I called in at the building society when I'd finished my shopping. I'd been putting it off, because I knew I would be shocked by the balance of my account. I was. I can hardly believe how much I've got through since the divorce.

I spent the afternoon trying to bloody meditate. It didn't work, of course, it never does, though at least I didn't see Michael on a mortuary slab, which is something, I suppose.

But I still can't help thinking how much better that £400 could have been spent.

Antimacassars and Outrageous Rumours

Jack is coming home tomorrow and I've got to decide whether I keep on seeing him or not. I mean, sex has been good for me, true, but having someone after what bit of money I have left, definitely wouldn't be. Which is why I am off to the shop to see Helena Chopin.

I know I shouldn't listen to anything Michael has to say, but on this occasion he may just have a point. It would explain why Jack has been so nice to me, well above and beyond the call of duty of a young man with a reputation to uphold. What do I really know about him, after all? Only that Nell thinks he is a good builder, and the things he has told me himself. And I reckon that if anyone can fill me in, then it's our local postmistress. I'm not at all sure what I'll say to her, how I shall broach the subject, but I expect I shall think of something.

It's a brilliantly sunny day as I set out from my house, and if I wasn't so confused about things, I'd probably feel very happy right now. I walk slowly to the shop, stop for a

148

while at the beck to watch the ducks, and wish I'd brought some bread with me so I could feed them. I realise again how lucky I am to live in such a pretty village.

I take a deep breath and head towards the shop again. I must get this over and done with. Only when I get there, I can see Helena turning the sign on the half glazed door from open to closed, and at the same time I hear the church clock strike one. It's lunchtime, and I can't decide whether I am relieved or disappointed. I start to walk away, but then I hear the shop door ping open and Helena calling out to me.

'Did you want something, love?'

I turn back to her. 'Just a paper and, well, maybe a bit of a chat. But it can wait.'

'Why don't you come in and have a cup of tea with me while I'm eating my lunch?'

I hesitate. I don't want this looking as if it's very important to me.

'Come on, love,' Helena is saying, 'I was hoping to have a word with you myself.'

So I smile and accept her invitation.

The room at the back of the shop is very small and jam-packed with ornaments. There's no room for a sofa, just two green Dralon-covered armchairs with antimacassars on their arms and headrests, and I am reminded of the house I grew up in.

She has me sit down on one of the armchairs and goes off into the kitchen to make the tea, which she does remarkably quickly.

'There we are,' she says, placing a tray of thick-cut sandwiches and two mugs of tea on the floor between us. 'Help yourself to a sandwich if you'd like one, but don't ask me what they are. Brian made them before he went to work.'

I decline but, since my mouth is very dry, I am grateful for the tea.

'So,' she says, eyeing one of the sandwiches a bit suspiciously, 'did you want a chat about anything in particular?'

'Not really,' I lie, 'just at a bit of a loose end.'

She takes a bite from her sandwich, and looks at me while she's chewing it. 'Nothing to do with that silly comment I made about Jack being a bit of a lad, then?'

Why does my body always let me down? Why do I turn the colour of a post-box whenever I am embarrassed?

She reaches over and touches my hand. 'Sorry, love. It's a small village. Things get around quickly here.'

I attempt a little laugh, but it comes out more like an hysterical sob. Damn and blast it.

She puts her plate back on the tray, picks up her mug. 'I was joking, love, honest I was, that's what I wanted to tell you. He's okay, is Jack. Known him since he moved into the village a couple of years ago, and I'll swear I've never heard a wrong word said about him.'

I sip my tea, not trusting myself to speak yet.

'All he needs to do is get his business on a good footing.'

I don't like the sound of that. I remember now what he said about needing money, which is why he had to take the job he is doing now. Which probably means he *is* after my money — or rather the money he thinks I've got — to tide him over until his business is on a good footing, whatever that means. God, I can't bear to think that Michael really was right.

'Trouble with Jack is that he's just too damn decent at times,' Helena's saying. 'He won't push for payments. He's a bit too willing to accept a good hard-luck story. He's owed a fair bit, I understand.'

Suddenly Helena is laughing. 'You'll have to forgive me, love, I probably shouldn't be telling you any of this. Brian is always saying I talk too much, and I expect he's right.'

'So Brian's your boyfriend, is he?' I say,

because I can't think of anything else to say.

She's hooting with laughter now. 'Brian, my boyfriend!' More hoots. 'Me and Brian.' She's shaking her head and hooting at the same time. 'No, love,' she manages at last, 'sorry to laugh like that, but I should have said when I introduced you to him. Brian's my brother, lived with me since his wife died a while back.'

I come away from Helena's more confused than ever and feeling a bit of a fool, as well.

★ ★ ★

Tomorrow has come and Jack will be home tonight, and I still haven't made a decision. I'm not so worried about the money thing now. I feel quite reassured by what Helena told me. It's the age difference which is worrying me again now. I don't want people sniggering at me behind my back. Maybe Michael is right, maybe it's okay for a man to be with a younger woman, but not the other way round. Or maybe that's just baloney.

I go into the kitchen, make blackcurrant tea, and as I'm lifting the bag out of the cup a letter drops on my doormat.

It's from Josephine Brown. Thanking me for my letter and telling me that she too would like to meet, but that she is going away for a while, to Canada — though she doesn't say why — and will contact me again when she returns. And she wishes me well, which makes me feel restless and angry, and I don't know why.

*   *   *

By twelve-fifteen, I have cleaned the house thoroughly and although I feel a little less restless and angry, I still can't decide about Jack. At two o'clock, I turn up at Kevin's salon and beg him to fit me in. He does, and then, when he's scrunch-drying my hair, he asks me if it's true, the rumour he's heard about me and some fabulous eighteen-year-old foreign waiter who is now living with me. I put him right as best I can, but I don't think he believes me.

I really must remember not to take all the gossip I hear from Kevin too seriously in future.

*   *   *

Three-thirty, and having finally plucked up the courage, I am sitting next to Harry's bed in Ward Three of the local hospital. He looks a bit drawn and he hasn't felt much like eating yet, but his spirits are remarkably high

153

for an eighty-two-year-old who has just been through major heart surgery. The present I bought for him is a collection of verse through the ages, and he tells me by the time he is released from hospital he is determined to have learned at least ten of the poems by heart.

★   ★   ★

Home again at five, and although I definitely feel a lot more cheerful, the fog in my mind still hasn't cleared.

★   ★   ★

I try calling Nell for advice, but she's out.

★   ★   ★

It's just after six when the telephone rings. I'm nervous about answering it in case it's Jack, but it turns out to be Hilary. She wonders if I'd like to bring *Keanu* to a party she's giving in a couple of weeks time. I ask her if Michael will be there and when she says that he will, I tell her I'm not sure of my plans, but I thank her again for dinner last week. I don't feel nearly so mad with Hilary now, not since Jack said she looked like Lily Savage.

Only she's reluctant to let me go.

'I thought he was absolutely charming, Anna,' she says about Jack. 'Charming *and* gorgeous. And it must be wonderful to get your own back on Michael like that. I must admit I feel quite envious of you. He hasn't got any good-looking friends, has he?'

And *I* must admit that it gladdens my heart to think of Hilary being envious of me.

And it's then, as I put down the receiver, that I finally make a decision. I will carry on seeing Jack. I will carry on seeing Jack because Hilary is envious of me, and because she's right about Michael. By continuing to see Jack, I will be getting my own back on him.

Not a very good reason, I know, but then I've made important decisions before on far less sound reasoning than that.

Delia Smith and
Home Improvements

We are into the second week of November now, it's the 12th, and like everyone else I am amazed by the continuing good weather. I have only had the central heating on three times so far this autumn. It must be saving me a small fortune.

It is mid-morning now, and I have just finished tidying the house. It's my birthday today and I have invited Nell and David to dinner this evening. Jack is coming early, because he knows I get into a panic about cooking, even for four. He offered to bring something special for pudding and I accepted without any argument.

Our relationship has moved on to a different level now. The sex is still great, but we're not at it all the time now. We do other things as well. I can pinpoint the day when things started to shift onto this new level. It was near the end of July. We were sitting in a pub garden, sipping cider and fighting off midges. We were laughing about something, I don't remember what, but all of a sudden it occurred to me that there I was, in public with Jack, and nobody was taking any special notice of us. It was like we were just an ordinary couple, instead of a young bloke and an older woman, and I began to relax. And I realised what fun I was having with Jack, out of bed as well as in it. I realised that we'd become friends.

After that, we started to do all sorts of things together. We took day trips to the coast — to Scarborough and Whitby, and went for long walks in the Dales. We scoured charity shops for bargains; we went to the cinema, to a few theatre productions; we hired videos, listened to music, and cooked meals for each other. I tried to teach him to swim at the local pool, he tried teaching me about gardening. We laughed a lot. We talked nonsense. We found solutions to the world's problems. We discovered irritating habits about one another, and forgave them.

The only thing I refused to do, was to meet Jack's parents, because, quite simply, I am a coward.

While all this was going on, I lost a bit of excess weight and my skin took on almost a Nell-like glow. All the good things which happen when *happy* chemicals are released into the system, happened to me. For the past few months, in fact, Jack has been the main focus of my life. I have given little thought to Michael, to Josephine Brown, to my dwindling finances, and never once has Jack made a play for my money. So I'm sure I did right to keep on seeing him.

I've kept the rest of the meal very simple and with Delia Smith's help it should be all right. Delia is my Number One role model. I admire her above all other women. It is her serenity, I think, which appeals to me most. That, and her ability to make every one of her huge television audience feel as if each demonstration is their own personal Master Class, by a very good friend. Some people I know think she seems a bit smug, but I don't understand that at all.

The telephone rings when I am rolling out ready-made puff pastry. I answer it with floury hands.

'Hi, Anna, how's it going?'

'Good, thanks, Nell, all under control.'

Like Jack, Nell knows I get worked up about cooking, and was all for us going to her house. But I was insistent.

Nell never gets in a panic about entertaining. Not because she is serene, like Delia, but because she cheats and buys everything pre-cooked from a woman she knows who makes a living from supplying delicious *home-made* food for the busy hostess.

There is a slight pause and I wonder what's up.

'Look, Anna, I don't like being the one to tell you, but I thought you'd probably prefer to hear it from me than anyone else. And we may not get the chance to talk about it tonight.'

God, I think, what now? But no ideas come into my head.

'It's Michael,' she says. 'I've heard he and Shelly are getting married.'

I am shocked by this, but I think it's mainly because Nell has used the ex-typist's real name. I mean, Michael and I have been separated nearly a year now so why should I care if he compounds his madness by marrying that half-baked trollop?

'Stupid old fool,' I say, because I am required to say something.

'My own thoughts precisely,' Nell says, and I can hear the relief in her voice.

★ ★ ★

I am well ahead of myself for a change, and decide I can spare a couple of hours with Harry. I hadn't planned going there today, but I've got this strong urge to see him.

When I pass by the turn off for my old home, I wonder if Michael ever tracked down the source of the smell in his bedroom. This makes me smile, for a moment, then I think: did I really do that? And did I really do all those other things, as well?

Harry looks quite his old self again these days, and his mind is as sharp as ever. As good as his word, he learnt at least ten poems from that book of verse, and I usually get him to recite one to me when I visit. I notice that most of the poems he's learnt are about love and loss and stuff like that. He's a real romantic, is Harry.

I wanted him to come to my birthday dinner but he says he doesn't like going out at night these days, so we've agreed to have lunch together sometime instead. We are getting close to finishing his book, so we've decided to make it a double celebration. There was quite a long period when Harry wasn't up to writing, but he's been slogging away solidly for a few weeks now and we're definitely getting there. Just one more chapter to type up, then some general editing, and it will be ready to send off to a publisher.

Harry is delighted to see me and when I thank him for the gorgeous bath oil and card he sent to me, he gives me a special birthday hug.

I tell him I want to get right down to work, that with a bit of luck I should get the last chapter finished today.

I do finish, and feel immensely pleased with myself. Pleased for Harry, as well, because I know how good his book is. Maybe I'm just biased, but I don't think so.

We are now drinking strong coffee together in Harry's kitchen, (I have given up giving up coffee and feel a lot better for it) and I tell Harry about Michael getting married. I think, if I'm completely honest, that's why I came here today.

'And how do you feel about that?' he asks, like he's a trained counsellor or something.

'I haven't made up my mind yet.' Which is true.

'You haven't seen much of Michael lately, have you?'

I shake my head. I haven't seen *anything* of Michael lately.Not since I told him to get lost, or words to that effect. I haven't even spoken to him on the telephone.

'And you seem a lot happier for it. Though I'm sure having Jack around helps as well.' He likes Jack, does Harry. He hasn't said as much but he doesn't need to, I can just tell.

'So what are you saying, Harry?'

'I'm saying that the best thing you can do is wish him well, Anna, and get on with your life.'

Which is good advice. Except that since I passed my old house earlier today, I keep thinking about how I spent most of the month of June trying to do away with Michael, and I'm finding it all very worrying.

⋆ ⋆ ⋆

I drink more than I should before Nell and David get here. They arrive on time and Nell looks stunning, as usual. David, who Hilary thinks looks a lot like a middle-aged Paul Newman, actually does a bit. By nature, he is almost as lively as Nell, and together they can be a bit much at times. But tonight, for them, they are not quite so robustly cheerful. I notice this immediately, and wonder if Nell has said something to David about Michael getting married and has asked him to behave sensitively. God, I hope not. I hate it when people treat me as if I am fragile.

'I hope you like it,' Nell says as I'm removing the wrapping paper from the gift she and David have brought for me. 'I thought you could put that picture of Megan and Brandon in it.'

I am amazed by the quality of the beautiful silver picture frame, and touched by Nell's thoughtfulness. It makes me feel alarmingly sentimental. I kiss them both, feel tears prick at my eyes, and then to prevent the flood gates opening, I get out the photo Nell was talking about. It arrived a couple of days ago, along with a silk scarf for my birthday.

'Good-looking couple,' David says, and I can feel my chest puffing with pride.

'Fabulous scarf,' says Nell. 'What did you get her, Jack?'

Jack glances at me and I try not to look embarrassed. He bought me some sexy underwear — tastefully sexy, which I am wearing now — but I do not feel inclined to share anything quite so personal, with David, anyway. So I lie and tell Nell that Jack is taking me out at the weekend so that I can choose something special.

I pour myself more wine and leave Jack to chat with David while I panic over the food in the kitchen, with Nell for support.

Now that I am alone with Nell, I have the feeling I'm expected to say something else about Michael getting married. I suspect that's why she followed me into the kitchen. I'm trying to think of something appropriate to say while I'm transferring the potatoes into a serving dish, only my hand is a bit shaky and I manage to miss the dish and spill most of them in the sink, which is full of soapy water.

'Bugger!'

Nell calmly lets the water out of the sink, rinses the soapy potatoes, and puts them in the serving dish. 'Nobody will be any the wiser,' she tells me, and I believe her.

'You seem very edgy tonight,' she says as she's watching me put the potatoes in the Rayburn with the other vegetables. 'I hope it hasn't got anything to do with Michael and Shelly.'

I look round at Nell. 'Must you keep calling her by her name?'

'Sorry. Has it got anything to do with Michael and the *extypist*, then?'

I feel a bit unsteady on my feet and it occurs to me that I've probably already got through the best part of a bottle of wine.

'Nothing at all,' I answer coolly. I take some plates out of the cupboard, wonder if there's room in the oven to warm them, decide there probably isn't.

'Have you told Jack yet?'

'Why should I tell him?'

'What's more to the point, why shouldn't you?'

'Why should or shouldn't you tell me what?' says Jack, who has just come into the kitchen.

An uncomfortable silence descends, and as Nell and I both turn towards Jack, David joins him and his presence somehow breaks the tension.

'Tell you later,' I say.

We eat in the dining room. Jack's idea, to make more of an occasion of the evening. We have a simple mixed leaf salad with a cheesy dressing for starters, then a fish pie *à la* Delia, for mains. Both go down well.

Now that my bit is out of the way, I can relax.

I can enjoy the performance Jack makes of the enormous meringue, which is his contribution tonight. He made it himself, which impresses everyone, and has piped *Happy Birthday Anna* a bit shakily on top of a chocolate coating. He has placed a single candle in the centre and with Nell in charge of lights, he puts a match to the candle and the three of them sing 'Happy Birthday' to me. It makes me think of another birthday and my silver cardboard key, and I pour wine for myself as Jack serves his meringue.

We talked about all sorts of things during the meal. About the state of the nation, a grisly local murder, Nell's recent conversion from aerobics to circuit training, the extraordinary weather, Jack's latest building job, David's work as an architect; and now, quite suddenly, as we are finishing Jack's excellent pudding, we are talking about Michael. David's fault.

He has apparently been asked to do some drawings for some conversion work on my old home, and once it had slipped out, nothing was going to stop me hearing about it. I pour more wine for us all and ask David what sort of conversion work he is talking about.

David glances at Nell and I can see that he is uneasy, that he wasn't supposed to have said anything.

Nell tries changing the subject. She tells me what a great job I've done in the dining room, but I ignore her.

'For God's sake, David, just tell me, will you.'

I'm aware of the tension in the room but I don't care about it. I just carry on glaring at David, waiting for him to answer my question.

He attempts a laugh, makes a joke about client confidentiality, and I tell him that he can stuff that. 'This is no ordinary client we are talking about, and anyway you're not a bloody doctor or lawyer.'

'It's nothing much,' he says, trying not to look at Nell now, 'just a bit of knocking around upstairs, so as to create an extra bathroom.'

I think about this. 'Well, the only way you could do that is to make one of the bedrooms smaller, and what's the point of that?'

Then I realise the point all by myself. A smaller bedroom would be just fine for a nursery and an extra bathroom would be very useful with a baby in the house.

'She's pregnant, isn't she?'

I say this to Nell, who would like to lie to me, I know, but can't, so she just nods instead.

God, why didn't she tell me all this when she phoned this morning? But I know why. She intended breaking it gently. Marriage first. Get used to that. Then the baby.

If I was sober, I would probably make some cruel crack about Michael right now and laugh about it. Only I've had loads to drink and I don't seem to care about putting my guests at their ease. Besides, Nell and David aren't just any old guests. They are my very good friends and I'm allowed to be myself with them.

Everyone is looking at me, waiting to see what I will say next. Jack is looking at me very intently, and I find myself wishing he wasn't here, because although he too is my friend, ours is a different sort of friendship, and I can't bring myself to say what I want to say in front of him, though I'm not even sure what that is.

'Anyone for coffee?' I say, because I have to say *something*, and I need to get out of the room.

I didn't let Jack stay last night and I know he is hurt by my coolness towards him. But I couldn't help it, and I was too sorry for myself to deal with his feelings as well as my own.

I get up with a headache and take a couple of aspirins. Serves me right for being such a lush.

I sit down at my kitchen table with the intention of paying some bills, to distract myself, but can't be bothered when it comes to it. So I push everything aside and reach for some writing paper. I prefer writing letters at my kitchen table to writing them at my desk. They seem to flow better. Or they usually do.

I write, *Dear Josephine*, scratch it out, then, *Dear Mrs Brown*.

★ ★ ★

Funny how she married someone with the first two letters of her own surname, I think, wondering if this was intentional. I decide this is a very silly idea, and get up from the table to hunt for the last letter she sent to me. I can't seem to recall how I addressed her before, so I need a reminder. I find what I'm looking for in the same drawer as the

168

engraving, which I still haven't had reframed. I note that she has signed it with her Christian name, so that's what I use.

Dear Josephine

I hope you're well, and that your trip to Canada was enjoyable. You said you would contact me when you returned and maybe I should have waited for you to get in touch, but as five months have passed now, I have been getting a little concerned. I really would like to meet up with you, and soon, if possible. You could come here, or I could drive down to see you. I will be happy to fit in with whatever suits you.

I sign it, seal it in an envelope, address it, stamp it. Then I walk into the village and post it, before I have a chance to change my mind.

I am pleased to say that Helena Chopin has become quite a good pal of mine now. She assures me that I am no longer the main subject of gossip in the village, which I regret a bit. Still, I can't be greedy. I must make way for fresher and juicier rumours, such as that of the vicar and the married, female verger who were seen together, in unexplained circumstances, in a hotel in the Lake District.

When I get back to the house, I phone Nell and apologise for last night. She rang me earlier but I didn't answer, because I thought that it might be Jack. She didn't leave a message but I dialled 1471, so I knew it was her.

'You don't have to apologise for anything,' Nell says. 'I should have told you everything earlier.'

'Maybe,' I say, 'but I just wish I hadn't drunk so much and made an idiot of myself.'

'We all do it at times.' Then, 'What happened after we left? With Jack? He seemed a bit quiet about it all.'

I confess how horrible I was to him. 'But he'll get over it,' I say. 'He's used to my moods by now. He puts it down to me being a Scorpio.'

Then I tell Nell about my letter to Josephine Brown.

'Why now?' she asks. 'After letting it drift for so long.'

Why indeed?

'No idea, if I'm honest. One minute I was thinking about paying some bills, the next I was writing to her.'

'Well, whatever the reason, I'm pleased you've done it. And now that you've told me I'll make sure you go through with it.' There is a bit of a pause, then: 'But only if you want me to, of course.'

We both laugh at this, then Nell asks me how I am feeling today, about Michael, now I've had time to think about things?

I focus on the kettle which is on the Rayburn. There are little bursts of steam coming out of the spout.

'All right, I suppose. I know I shouldn't really care anymore, but, well, you know he never wanted any more kids after Megan, so perhaps it's only natural I should feel a bit hurt now that he's apparently changed his mind.'

'I can see that.'

'And not just for me, but for Megan, too. I didn't like being an only child myself and I'd have loved her to have a brother or sister.'

'The word is that she tricked him into it,' Nell says, to make me feel better, I suppose.

'Really,' she insists. 'I had it from *Jerry Hall* that *Kim Basinger* told her what she was up to. They're very chummy, those two. Only not so chummy as *Kim* would like to believe, or *Jerry* wouldn't be telling everyone.'

This cheers me a bit, makes me feel better for Megan, at least.

'You know Megan's coming home for Christmas,' I say. She is bringing Brandon with her so I have to assume it really is serious. 'Do you think I should warn her, or should I leave that to her idiot father?'

'I think he should tell her, only knowing him he probably won't. Perhaps you should have a word with him about it.'

Perhaps I should.

★ ★ ★

I telephone Jack and tell him I'm sorry. I ring him on his mobile phone, where he's working. He sounds a bit distant: punishing me, I expect, for sending him home last night. I ask him to come around tonight, not just because I want to show him how sorry I am, but because I want very much to have sex with him. He tells me he's not sure. He tells me he will probably be working quite late, and had planned on having an early night.

I tell him to do what he bloody well likes and put the phone down, hard.

Arum Lilies and
Brilliant Brainwaves

I find a bunch of flowers on my doorstep
when I collect the milk. They are the sort of
flowers husbands buy for their wives from
petrol stations when they're late home from
work without a good reason: gaudy, unnatural
coloured chrysanthemum sprays wrapped in
a stiff see-through film which is almost
impossible to remove. Attached is a card from
Jack, apologising for the flowers, and for
being so immature.

I notice, incredibly, that the roses around
my door are still going strong and that it is
yet another mild day. Will winter never come?

I have made up my mind to ring Michael
today but it has been so long since I have
spoken to him that I find I am putting it off,
looking for, and finding, other things to do.
It's hard to know what to say to him, and to
say it without resentment.

I'm going over to Harry's as usual this
afternoon, but that still leaves me with two
hours to kill. So I go for the ultimate
displacement tactic and take myself out. I

decide on the Hockney Gallery at Salt's Mill, because I love the arum lilies and the interesting books they have on sale there.

I read quite a lot these days. I have Jack to thank for this. He thought I watched too many soap operas, so he kept buying me books and reading the first chapter to me, so it got me interested and wanting to know what happened next. And once I got into reading, I found that I liked it and started buying books for myself. And I realised recently that I haven't watched a soap opera for ages.

There aren't many people in the gallery; a bit early yet, I suppose. There are two young people at the pay desk, discussing a grievance one of them seems to have about her hours of work. I try not to listen while I am browsing. The scent of lilies is not so strong today, or perhaps my senses are not so sharp.

I find myself in the Personal Growth section, and flick through some of the books with their wildly inspirational titles. I like the look of some of them but not enough to buy one. So I move on to the novels and after a while settle on a book about a woman who kills her husband, only it looks as if she does it while she's still married to him.

Then I wander around the gallery, take in

the twenty-foot potted plants, the cathedral-like feel of the building which was once a working mill, and I have a smile to myself at Hockney's Dachshunds. Is he having us on, or are we being invited to share the joke?

'Anna! What on earth are you doing here?'

I would know that gushing voice anywhere. I manage to fix a smile on my face as I turn to greet Hilary.

I try to keep the smile going when I see the ex-typist standing next to her. I've never met her before, but I know it's her straight way. I know it by the glee on Hilary's face.

'You two do know one another, of course,' she says without the slightest trace of discomfort. I find it hard not to look at Shelly, and when I do, I note she at least has the good grace to appear awkward. And she doesn't look remotely like Kim Basinger, I decide.

Hilary's eyes scan us both and come to rest on Shelly's abdomen. She looks disappointed at the absence of any visible evidence of the pregnancy. She is probably wondering how to bring it up without sounding too obvious.

So I decide to save her the trouble.

'I believe congratulations are in order,' I say to Shelly, sounding incredibly matter-of-fact. I even manage to widen my smile.

Shelly looks taken aback. All sorts of emotions cross her face in an instant: surprise, suspicion, confusion, pleasure. But it is Hilary's expression I will treasure. There are no confused emotions here. There is only annoyance that someone got to me before she did.

'When is the baby due?' I ask, amazed at my calm and how pleasant I sound.

'Not until April,' Shelly says, in that squeaky little voice that I have only heard on the telephone until now.

'How nice,' I say, 'a spring birth.'

'Yes,' Shelly says, suspicion and confusion all but gone now. 'Just so long as it's not born on the first of the month,' she quips. This comes out so easily I imagine it is a long-standing joke. One of Michael's, I should think. About his standard, anyway.

'We're going upstairs for coffee,' Hilary announces. 'Would you like to join us, Anna?' Clearly she has still not entirely given up on the chance of a bit of amusement at my and Shelly's expense.

'I'd love to, Hilary, but you know, things to do, people to see.' I am parodying her own sillyspeak, but I am wasting my time as she is clearly completely unaware of the fact. My body language would inform most people that I am trying to take my leave, but Hilary seems ignorant to this most basic of all human language.

'And how is that gorgeous young hunk of yours, Anna? Word has it he is still very much on the scene. I've heard the two of you might even beat Michael and Shelly to the altar.'

I decide it would not be a good move to tell Hilary what to do with herself, though it is sorely tempting.

'I can't imagine where you hear such things, Hilary,' I say instead. 'I much prefer having a lover to a husband, any day. I find them so much more attentive and willing to please.'

I feel a bit guilty about this, talking about Jack as if he is some sort of sexual plaything. But needs must.

Shelly giggles at this and, amazingly, I find myself actually warming to her; feeling sorry for her because she will have to put up with Michael, in marriage, as I had done for so long. It makes me shudder now to think that I might have stayed with Michael for the rest of my life, that I *would* have stayed with him had it not been for Shelly. And to think that only a couple of days ago I was upset because they were getting married, miserable because Shelly was having his baby. I wish that I'd met Shelly long ago. Because meeting her now has changed things. In my mind, despite all the mean things I have thought and said about her, she remained some sort of wicked *femme fatale* who probably took pleasure from ruining lives. But now, as I look at this fairly ordinary young woman, my feelings towards her are very nearly tender, almost sisterly, in fact.

Hilary looks suitably peeved by my remark and after one long sweep of her eyes over me — a look which says: *How the hell does she do it?* — she ushers Shelly away in a manner which can only be described as predatory, which makes me feel sorry for Shelly all over again.

*   *   *

Jack is waiting on my doorstep when I get back from Harry's.

'I'm sorry for being such an idiot,' he says, as I put the key in my lock.

'Me too,' I tell him.

I heat up something for us both in the microwave, and we drink cheap wine and talk about his current job. I'm on to cheap wine now because I am becoming more sensible about money. A case of having to. It is amazing how quickly my capital is disappearing.

'I'm thinking about doing something,' I tell him, suddenly.

'What sort of something?' he asks, his fork half-way to his mouth.

'Starting a business.' I am saying it exactly as it comes into my head. I swear no such thought had entered my mind until this very moment, but it comes out like I've been planning it for ages.

'I'm going to open an antiques shop,' I tell him. 'I'm going to go to auction sales, like I used to, and start collecting things so I'll have enough to fill the shop when I find suitable premises. I think I have developed an eye for a good buy over the years.'

I say all this with the sort of confidence I only usually have when I'm drunk.

Before Jack has a chance to respond to my brilliant idea, the telephone rings. I take it in the sitting room because I know, I am absolutely certain, that it is Michael. Shelly will have told him about our meeting this morning; he will probably be pleased that I was so nice to her. He will probably think it is safe to speak to me again.

'Anna,' he says, 'how could you?' I am surprised with this opening.

'How could I what?'

'How could you say all that crap about preferring lovers to husbands. You don't

179

impress anyone with that sort of talk. It's so bloody pathetic.'

I forget all my good intentions and feel murderous towards him again for the first time in ages. The only way I can deal with the feeling is to ignore what he's said.

'I'm glad you rang,' I tell him, coolly. 'I think you should write to Megan and tell her what's happening.'

He is obviously off-balanced by this. It is not the response he expected.

'I've already done it,' he says, only I know he is lying.

'Good,' I say. 'You owe her that much, at least. Is that it, then?'

'Not quite. I wondered if you'd like the dogs back.'

I'm not sure I understand him correctly. So I ask what he means.

'I think they miss you,' he says, 'and I've always thought of them as your dogs, really.'

This is rich, really rich.

'So why didn't you let me have them when I left? You told me they were better off staying in the house they knew, and I accepted that. So what's changed?'

'Nothing's changed. I'm just trying to do the right thing.'

Then it hits me. 'What you mean is that it no longer suits you to keep the dogs now

180

there is going to be a baby in the house.' I remember well how Michael objected to pets when Megan was born. I wanted a dog then, but he wouldn't hear of it. He has the idea that babies and pets don't mix.

'Okay,' I say, because I'm too weary to say what I'm really thinking. And anyway, I want the dogs. I want them more than anything at this very moment. But I am not grateful to Michael. Not at all. And I refuse to pretend that I am.

'When do you want to bring them round?'

'Would tomorrow suit you?'

'No, it bloody well wouldn't suit me. I'll have them at the end of the week.'

'Fine,' he says, and then puts the phone down.

★　★　★

Jack stayed the night and things were just great until he told me he loved me.

★　★　★

Nell is surprised to see me, but pleased. I don't usually turn up at her house without calling her first. She leads such a busy life that I think myself lucky to find her in. As it is, I only just manage it. She is all set for an hour at her gym but doesn't mind putting it off for a while.

She pours pear juice for both of us and we sit in her brightly decorated kitchen.

Hers is a beautiful house, a happy mix of old-world charm and David's clever architectural skills. And it's big. Huge, in fact. Far too big for just the two of them and a lazy Blue Persian cat called Billy.

'You look like a woman with something on her mind,' Nell says, like a woman with very little other than the next workout on hers.

Billy, the Blue Persian is purring and pummelling my lap, trying to get comfortable. I stroke his long hair and he starts to purr louder and pummel harder. 'It's Jack,' I say, 'he told me he loved me last night.'

Nell looks less amazed than I expected her to. But she is frowning. 'I'm not sure what you want me to say. If I'm surprised at all it's only to learn that the 'L' word hasn't been mentioned before. It's obvious that Jack thinks the world of you.'

'Yes, as a friend, sure. And well . . . for certain other things, maybe.'

'Don't be coy, Anna, it doesn't suit you.'

'Okay, so we get on well together in bed.'

'Well, what else is there, for goodness sake? Good friends and good lovers. Crikey, Anna, you've got it made.'

Billy has finally settled down, is curled in a tight ball in my lap. I feel a bit exasperated. Nell isn't getting this. 'But it's messed things up, don't you see? I don't want Jack telling me he's in love with me. I preferred things before, I knew where I was then.'

'God, Anna, sometimes I despair of you, I really do.' And she looks despairing, as well, which is worrying. But maybe it's because I'm not explaining myself very well.

'And what about the timing?' I say, trying again. 'How come he's talking about love just when he hears Michael is getting married again?'

She lets out a sigh. 'Like I said, I'm surprised he hasn't said something before, but if he hasn't there was probably a very good reason. I dare say he suspected you weren't ready for it, but now ... well, I imagine he thinks the timing *is* good, good for you, that is. Most women would be feeling pretty vulnerable when they hear their 'ex' is getting married again, they'd be glad to hear that another man loves them.'

'Yeah, but I'm okay about that now.' I tell her about bumping into Shelly and Hilary, and how sorry I felt for Shelly. 'I can even use her name now, which must mean something.'

'Did you explain any of this to Jack?'

'Well, no, but ... '

'But what? Is he supposed to be a mind reader, or what?'

'No, yes, but you're missing the point. Like I said, I preferred things the way they were before. I just don't want all that emotional stuff.'

Nell looks at me for a while without smiling. 'It's all about *you*, isn't it, Anna? Maybe you should try thinking about Jack and *his* feelings for a change.'

★　★　★

Which is more or less how we left it. I was so hurt by Nell's remarks that I made my excuses soon after that and left. I didn't even tell her about starting a business.

So when I go to see Harry, I tell him about it instead. I begin with my money worries, and how I'd dismissed the idea of getting a job because I can't do anything, except type a bit, but I can't even do that well enough to earn a living from it. (And to think how mean I was about Shelly, who did manage to earn a living from her typing.) 'Which doesn't really leave that many options,' I say. 'I could blow everything I've got left on lottery tickets, I suppose, or I could do something just a little less risky, and start a business.'

'I presume you have something specific in mind?' Harry says.

I tell him about my antiques idea, and he seems to like it. Which is more than Jack did. All he did was point out the pitfalls.

When I've more or less told Harry everything, he gives me one of his wise looks. 'There's more to this than a need to provide an income, isn't there, Anna?'

And he's right, there is. I realised something quite important recently. I realised why I let Michael take so many of my things without a fight. I let him take them because I believed he had more right to them than I did, because it was *his* money which paid for them. I didn't really believe I was entitled to anything, and if I'm ever to take control of my life, then I must prove to myself that I am.

I get stuck into Harry's book and find that the editing goes particularly well today. Harry sits beside me while I work, and we discuss which bits should be left in and which should be taken out. We seem to agree on most things.

One more week, I tell him, and it should be ready for posting.

★   ★   ★

There is a message on my answerphone from Josephine Brown. Her voice sounds very strange to me and I find myself playing the message back over and over. She has a peculiar accent, part Midland, part Irish. At least, I assume that is the mixture, by my limited knowledge of her, but if I did not know better I would think it was American.

The message is not a long one. It is like the letters she sent to me, tantalisingly lacking in detail. 'Hello, dear,' she begins, and this seems especially odd to me, the *dear* bit. I cannot recall anyone ever calling me that before, except for the odd elderly shop assistant.

'*Hello, dear, this is Josephine Brown. Thank you for your letter. I was going to write back, but thought it might be easier if we spoke on the telephone. Perhaps you could call me later. I'll be in all evening.*' (Then she tells me her number.) '*Well then, goodbye, dear. I'll look forward to hearing from you.*'

It is a very weird experience hearing for the very first time the voice of the woman who gave birth to me. I try to conjure up an image to go with the voice but all I can manage is an older version of myself. Not that it's easy to add years to my own image. I find myself

186

looking in the bathroom mirror with far greater interest than usual, trying to picture a few extra lines here, some additional sagging there. It is a rather pointless exercise but it keeps me occupied for ages.

Friendly Green Doors and Tuna Sandwiches

I'm glad I asked Jack not to come round tonight. I told him I needed some time to think about things on my own. And I have been thinking about things, about him, and in particular about the 'L' word. I've been thinking about it as I sit here on my own, trying to pluck up the courage to ring Josephine Brown. I've tried taking Nell's advice, about considering Jack's feelings in this, but it keeps coming back to me and what I want, and what I want is to be my own person, and I can't do that if I start getting all emotional about Jack. I know what will happen if I do, I'll get lazy and let him take over and then it will be just like it was with Michael.

Damn Jack for spoiling everything. Because now I shall just have to finish things with him, and I shall miss having him around.

I drink the last of my whisky before making the call to Josephine Brown. My heart is beating incredibly fast as I listen to the ringing tone. I am half hoping she's out, after all — called away urgently to see a sick friend. Then I think, God, what if there is a *Mr* Brown, and he answers the phone? What if he doesn't know about me? What if I'm a ghastly secret from his wife's murky past? But then, I think, if there *was* a Mr Brown who doesn't know about me, why would she have given me her number? I relax a bit, but just to be on the safe side I make up my mind to pretend I've got a wrong number if a man does answer.

'Hello,' the voice I recognise from the answerphone says.

'Oh, hello, it's me.'

What an utterly ridiculous thing to say, *me* could be just about anyone. But she knows who me is straight away.

'How lovely to hear your voice at last, dear.' She sounds nice. Very nice. I find myself suddenly on the verge of tears.

'Nice to hear you, too,' I manage to say.

There is a pause now, an uncomfortable one, and I wonder if I should jump in again and say something else.

'There's so much I want to say to you,' she tells me at last, 'but I think I'd prefer to do it face to face. What do you think, dear?'

'I think you're right,' I say, only I don't really think this at all. I want to ask at what time of day I was born, how long I spent with her before I was taken away, whether or not she cried when I'd gone, if she thought of me on my birthdays, and most of all, why the fuck she gave me away in the first place. And I want to know it all now.

'You made a number of possible suggestions in your letter,' she is saying. 'Well, if you don't mind very much, it would be better for me if you came here. I don't drive, you see, and I get a bit flustered with public transport.'

Silly cow, I am thinking, because she sounds so weak and pathetic and I don't want her to sound like that.

'Of course I don't mind,' I say. 'When would suit you best?'

'Any day next week — would Thursday be all right?'

'Thursday would be fine.'

'I'll send you a map,' she adds, 'with directions on how to get here.'

I thank her for this and say how much I am looking forward to meeting her at long last, then I put down the phone and amazingly, cry till I'm sick.

★ ★ ★

Nell is very excited for me when I tell her my news. She says she's sorry for being so hard on me about Jack, and I tell her not to give it another thought, though I'm still a bit miffed with her.

* * *

Jack seems excited for me as well, but then goes and spoils things again by offering to drive me to Solihull. The quicker I tell him it's over the better.

* * *

I think about phoning Megan, telling her about Josephine Brown, which for some reason I haven't done before. But in the end I decide against it.

* * *

Today, Wednesday, I parcel up Harry's manuscript and post it off to the first publisher on the list we made together. I thought about photocopying it and sending it off to a number of publishers at the same time, but I have heard somewhere that this is not good practice.

Harry is as happy as a boy with a new bicycle (his own expression) at the sight of the thick padded brown envelope.

We drink strong coffee, with double cream, and talk about how he will spend his first million. It starts off as a joke, with preposterous ideas, but then it gets serious with serious suggestions coming from both of us. Then a big grin appears on Harry's face, which makes me laugh and realise how carried away we were getting.

A funny thing about Harry is that I have never, in the whole of the time I have known him, heard him laugh out loud.

*　*　*

Later, I get out the engraving that Michael wanted from me way back in June, and look at it closely again. As if my sudden decision to deal in antiques will have made me an instant authority. It hasn't. I am still as ignorant as ever as to its meaning. I leave it out, on the kitchen table, determined to get the damn thing reframed, before I run out of money completely.

I spend the evening mulling over Premises To Let, to take my mind off the journey tomorrow, and what I will find at the end of that journey. I think about making a list of things to ask Josephine Brown but I decide against it. I've had the questions so long in my mind that a list isn't necessary. But I'm nervous, so nervous I almost give in and ring Jack. Instead, I drink coffee and eat five chocolate biscuits, the combined caffeine in them all guaranteeing to keep me awake all night.

* * *

I set out at six, while it is still dark, and arrive in Solihull at a quarter to ten: which is good for someone who hates long distance driving as much as I do. It is only now that I realise how close Solihull is to my childhood home. No more than thirty miles, at a guess. That has to mean something, surely.

There is a light mist over the town which makes it look grey and dismal. I get out the map Josephine Brown duly sent to me, and try and get my bearings. It is a remarkably detailed map and I have no real difficulty finding the street she lives in. It is quite a smart street, wide, with trees, and behind them, biggish Victorian houses.

Josephine Brown's house, number twenty-two, looks no less smart than the other houses in the street. It does not have a drive, as such, but a fairly long pathway leading to steps, which in turn lead to a green-painted door. I read somewhere that green doors mean friendly occupants, which cheers me a bit.

I note on my trudge up the pathway that the garden is still remarkably colourful for November. But there has been no frost to speak of so far, so nothing has yet been killed off. I find myself, stupidly, looking for a yellow rose bush, as if love of certain flora might be genetically inherited. I know this is a nonsense, but I am still disappointed not to find one.

I cannot see a doorbell to ring so I use a lion-faced knocker which has been painted over in green. The sound it makes is very deep and echoey.

Like the recent two minute silence to remember the war dead, it seems a very long time before the door is finally opened. During the period between knocking on the door and the first sounds on the other side of it, I thought of escape at least three times. But now, as the door slowly opens, I can think only of my shallow breath and the speed that my heart is racing, and, like any self-respecting hypochondriac, I convince myself I am on the verge of a heart attack.

The gap in the door widens and so do my eyes as I take in the figure standing there in the entrance.

She looks about sixty, far too young to be the mother of a forty-five-year-old. She is shorter than I am by about four inches. She is wearing smartish clothes, a navy blue woollen suit, that screams Genteel Respectability, and makes me feel uncomfortable about my jeans — why didn't I dress up? She has greying hair, but there is still quite a lot of dark to be seen. She has green eyes, greener than mine. She is quite pretty, if sixty-year-olds can be described as pretty. She has small, pleasant features, and she looks like someone who would call people *dear*. I decide there and then that I must look like my father.

I'd rehearsed this moment often in the car. I'd been through many versions of how it would be: her, taking me in her arms and hugging me; me, seeing that she is shy, taking her in my arms; the two of us rushing into one another's arms; the two of us bursting into happy tears.

But none of these things happen. Instead, after quite a long time just looking one another over, she holds out her hand to me. Mechanically, I offer mine in return and, to my amazement, she shakes it.

'It's good of you to come all this way, dear,' she is saying, 'won't you come in?'

So I follow her into the dimly lit house in a state of semi-shock. This isn't how it is supposed to be at all.

She shows me into the first room off the wide hallway. It is quite pleasantly furnished with odd pieces of antique furniture that I suspect are probably quite valuable.

She asks if I would prefer tea or coffee, and I go for the coffee. I'm tired after a sleepless night and a long drive and I need something to keep me alert.

Both forms of beverage are ready and waiting on a low table, which I find surprising. How could she have known exactly when I would arrive? Or maybe she has been making fresh tea and coffee at quarter-hour intervals all morning.

I sit as I am bid on a plump, button-back Victorian armchair. It is covered in burgundy coloured velvet and it looks like a chair which is not used very often. The fire is lit in the grate, though it, and an overhead light with its low wattage bulb, do little to relieve the gloom of the room and the gloom I am feeling.

'You must tell me all about yourself,' Josephine Brown says to me, like someone asking for the ingredients of a recipe, because that is the polite thing to do.

'I'd rather hear about you first,' I say.

She sighs a little in response, then, between sips of tea from a pink rose-patterned china teacup, she does indeed tell me about herself. About how tragic her life has been. About the 'shame' of having me when she was just sixteen years old, about the 'unkindness' of the Irish nuns in the home she was sent to, about being 'forced' to come to England when she was seventeen, to escape the shame, about her 'unfortunate' marriage to an Englishman called Peter Brown at nineteen, about being 'bullied' into moving to Canada when she was just twenty-one (which explains the accent), about the 'painful' births of the two children of that marriage, about being left 'penniless' after her husband's early death, about the 'ingratitude' of her offspring as they grew up, about her 'unhappy' return to an England she no longer cared for, about the 'struggle' she had and still has to make ends meet, to keep such a big, greedy house on such a low income, and finally, about her recent, 'disappointing' visit to her children in Canada.

By the time she finishes, hardly stopping to draw breath between each catastrophic event in her life, I have come to the conclusion that I dislike Josephine Brown, or Brady, or whoever the hell she is, intensely. One ray of hope still remains, however. What if her whole miserable life was the result of losing me?

'But what about me?' I ask her, the weak, foul-tasting coffee now cold in my cup. 'How did you feel about having to give me up?'

She looks at me in surprise, with her head a

little on one side, as if she has not quite understood the question. Then the penny drops suddenly and her face becomes vaguely animated again. Animated with self-pity.

'There was no question of keeping you, dear. How could a sixteen-year-old, still really a child herself, possibly look after a baby?'

I am immensely irritated with this move of hers into the third person, as if she is talking about someone other than herself.

'But did you never even consider it?' I have moved to the edge of my seat and perhaps I look, or sound, threatening, because I notice that she has begun to look nervous. But I don't much care about her feelings. If she didn't feel anything about giving me up, then I am just praying that she will lie, at least pretend that she felt something.

'I'm sure I did, dear, but it was taken out of my hands, it simply was not the done thing to keep illegitimate children in Ireland, certainly not then, anyway. Though I expect things have changed now. There's been so much change everywhere lately.'

I sense that she is about to start on some other woeful event in her life, so I cut in fast before she gets the chance.

'Can you remember the time of my birth?' I ask her, and she looks surprised again.

'Not really, dear, though I do remember

that you were born on a Sunday. I remember it because of the verse: you know, . . . but the child that is born on the Sabbath Day is . . . '

I interrupt her again. 'Do you remember the date?' She must remember the bloody date.

She looks vaguely off into the flames of her inadequately fed fire. 'I know it was winter. It was miserable weather at the time, I recall.'

'Don't you even remember which month it was?'

She presses her lips together hard, then her eyes light up, and she looks triumphant. 'It was November, somewhere near the middle of November. Around this very time, come to think of it.'

She looks back at me, pleased with herself, apparently.

'I have only one more question for you,' I tell her, and she smiles at me. A smile of relief, I suspect.

'And what would that be, dear?'

I think to myself that if she calls me *dear* just one more time I might very well scream.

I lean forward and look into her foggy, far-off eyes.

'Who was my father?'

★ ★ ★

I drive north through a deepening mist, feeling almost as sorry for myself as Josephine Brown did for herself.

When I get home I ring Jack. I need him to tell me that the Nature Argument is rubbish.

But he isn't in. It's only four, so he is probably still at work. I try his mobile, but find it's switched off. I want to cry. I'm not sure whether this is due to misery or frustration, or both. But I won't give in to it.

So I ring Nell, and David tells me she is circuit training. He says she'll be back soon, that she is dying to know how I got on with my mother, but I need someone now, and David just won't do.

There's only one other person left that I want to see, so I get in my car again and drive over to Harry's. He knows nothing about Josephine Brown and I won't speak to him of her now, but I just need his company.

I must look strange because he looks concerned.

'Would you like some tea, Anna? I have a pot on the go.'

I nod and let him pour me a cup and then follow him into the sitting room.

I drink the tea thirstily and stare at the fire, which is generous and lively, not mean and cheerless like Josephine Brown's.

'You look tired, Anna,' Harry says.

'I am. I've been driving all day.' And then, despite my decision not to tell him about Josephine Brown, I tell him everything, or almost everything. And if Harry is not surprised, because hardly anything surprises Harry, he is very perceptive. He knows when he is not being told the whole story.

I watch him struggle from his armchair.

'I'll be back in a moment,' he says, then leaves the room. He returns a few minutes later with more tea for me and a tuna fish sandwich.

'Eat that first, then tell me the rest.'

So I do eat because I am hungry and I never go off my food, however upset I am. And when I have eaten, I feel a bit better. I drain the contents of my cup and look at Harry.

'It was all very unpleasant when I left,' I tell him. 'I was really very rude to her.'

'Then I expect she deserved it. What did she say to you that made you want to be rude?'

I'm not sure about this. I am afraid to say it because saying it might make it real. But I say it anyway.

'I asked her about my father.'

'And?'

'She said she was raped.'

Harry is silent for a while and when I look

at him he has his eyes closed. Then he opens them and looks at me, really looks at me.

'You had every right to be rude to her, Anna, and if she was here now I would be rude to her as well. She had no business to say that to you even if it was true, which I doubt very much.'

'But what if it is true?'

'I don't see how it makes any difference at all. But I don't think it is. From how you've described Mrs Brown, I think that is just the sort of thing that she would say. She is just refusing to take responsibility for becoming pregnant with you as she refuses to take responsibility for everything else in her life.'

I like that. It makes sense, and for a moment I am relieved. But only for a moment. Because then it occurs to me that Harry doesn't know me as well as he thinks he does. He thinks of me as this pleasant sort of woman who helps him with his work, and tells him how wonderful he is all the time. He doesn't know that I am criminal, that I twice attempted to kill my ex-husband, that I got *him* to supply the poison I used in the second attempt, that he could himself have ended up dead at my wicked hands.

And maybe I am wicked because of my genes. Genes I have inherited from my rapist father.

I think about confessing everything, telling Harry the sort of person I really am but I can't bear to see the expression on his face, so I pretend instead that he's right.

'You're right,' I say. 'She's probably lying and if she isn't, how could it possibly matter?'

New Picture Frames and Faggots in Gravy

It is the last day in November and the frost has come at long last. It has killed off my roses and various blossoms in the garden which arrived prematurely, in their belief that spring had come early. Nature, like me, has been very confused this year. There is a lot of greyness about now, but the evening sunsets remain spectacular. There is no month like November for spectacular sunsets.

Jack is cooking a meal for me at the moment, something vegetarian for a change. I am sitting by my ingle-nook fireplace with a huge fire blazing in the hearth. The dogs are asleep at my feet, and Judd, the big yellow labrador, is dreaming. He keeps making small yelping sounds and his legs are rigid, as if he is running away from, or after something, in his dream. Rusty, the old mongrel, is so still he looks dead. He always looks that way when he's asleep, so I am not remotely concerned about him.

It's all very cosy and as I listen to Jack clattering about in the kitchen, I cannot imagine feeling more content than I do now. Happiness, I read somewhere, is not wanting to be anywhere else at a particular moment. So at this very moment, I know what happiness is.

Jack comes into the room and gives me a glass of the red wine, which he brought with him. It's a bit rough, I suppose, but it's fine by me and I'm just grateful that Jack isn't a wine snob.

The sound of his voice wakens Judd from his dream and he looks up at Jack, then me, is reassured, and falls back immediately into a less troubled sleep.

'Should be about twenty minutes,' Jack says of the meal, then sits down on the sofa beside me.

I wish I could be as casual as he is when I cook.

I curl up close to him and sip my wine.

'Did I tell you Megan and Brandon are arriving on 23rd December?' I say this knowing full well that I have told him. 'She called yesterday to confirm.' She knows about Michael's marriage and the baby now and has accepted it reasonably well. I'm sure having Brandon helps. Like having Jack around helps me. Nell was so right about everything. What more could I want than a good friend and a good lover? I must have been crazy to think about ending such a relationship.

Jack smiles at me and nods. 'You seem very happy tonight, Anna. Do we have Megan to thank for that?'

'That, and the decision I've come to. It really is a weight off my mind.'

'You're sure, then?'

'Absolutely. It was a dumb idea anyway. What do I know about business? I'd probably have been bankrupt within the year.'

'I don't know about that, I'm sure you'd have made a good go of it.'

I think of my conversation with Harry not very long ago, and how proving I could do something for myself had seemed so important. But I can't think about that now, because it will only make me feel foolish and useless, and what is the sense in that?

'Besides,' I say, 'if you moved in here with me, I wouldn't need to worry so much about money.'

He was stroking my hair when I was speaking but now he has stopped. His body is a little tense, but I expect it is just the surprise. There has been no talk of Jack moving in here with me before. But there has been lots of other talk, ever since I told Jack about Josephine Brown and my rapist father. He was really sweet about it, just like Harry,

206

and Nell too, when I told her. He said he didn't believe it for a moment, and then he said that he loved me again and would be there for me whenever I needed him.

And since then I have needed him, a lot, and he's been as good as his word, and a few days ago I told him I loved him as well, and it feels nice and safe to love and to be loved.

But he doesn't make any response to my comment, so I tell him something about my conversation with Megan that I know I haven't mentioned before.

'I told Megan about you,' I say, because I know he'll be pleased.

'And?'

'I thought she might not take it too well, you know, because of her father and Shelly, and you being younger and everything, but she was fine about it. She was surprised, no doubt about it, but mostly I think she was glad.'

'Good,' he says, and although I can't see his face I can hear the smile in his voice. 'I was beginning to think I might have to keep out of the way while she was here.'

I was beginning to think the same thing, which is why I plucked up the courage and told her.

'I've got something for you,' Jack says, and I sit up straight so that he can get up from the sofa. He disappears into the kitchen and comes back with something flat and oblong shaped, wrapped in brown paper. It looks like a thin book or a picture.

He watches me as I tear off the paper. The sound has woken the dogs. They are sat up close to me now, looking eager, hopeful that the package contains something for them.

I let the paper fall to the floor for them to sniff at, and look at the picture with amazement. *My engraving*, in a new, chunky gold frame.

'It's lovely,' I say, as I examine the scene closely again. It looks slightly different now in its smart new frame. The figures seem more alive somehow, more real. The effect is heightened by the flickering firelight and the pinky glow in the room. I'm tempted to start trying to make some sense of it all again, only I'm feeling too happy right now to be bothered.

The dogs have been watching us hopefully but very politely as we ate Jack's delicious Lentil Thingy, as he called it, so I reward them both with a chunk of herb bread when we've finished, because it's all that is left.

As Jack is clearing the plates away, I am reminded, quite out of the blue, of my parents' strange diet, which was mostly faggots in gravy, because they were cheap and tasty and because they went so well with my father's potatoes, especially when they were fluffily mashed. I almost smile at the memory but then I check myself, because as it turned out, faggots in gravy may very well have been my parents' unlikely undoing.

It was about a month after my twenty-first birthday party, when I had a call from my parents' next-door neighbour to tell me that my father had died of a heart attack while eating faggots. I have no idea why she mentioned the faggots. I mean, why didn't she just say, 'while he was eating'? Why mention the circumstances at all, come to think of it? It was very odd, that, and I can only think that maybe she disapproved of faggots, and perhaps blamed my dad's death on his poor diet. And maybe she was right.

I went home to comfort my mother but she was not to be comforted. She died of cancer three months later, and I married Michael a month after that.

Strange, that I haven't thought about it all for such a long time, and stranger still that I should think about it now, when I was feeling so happy.

Jack has made my favourite pudding, a banana concoction, but I can't seem to face it now.

'I had a phone call from Michael,' Jack says when we've been silent for about five minutes.

I am astonished at this. I hardly know how to respond.

'When?' is all I manage to get out.

'Last night, late.'

'What did he want?'

'He asked me if I would like to submit an estimate for the work he's having done in the house.'

'I thought architects usually did that sort of thing, contact builders, I mean.'

'They do.' He pauses, then adds, 'He sounded drunk to me.'

I am at a loss again. I am completely mystified and simply shrug.

'He asked if I would like to go over to his house tomorrow morning, at nine.'

'You said no, I hope.'

Jack looks sheepish and I know he didn't say no.

'I could do with the work,' he says, only I know there is more to it than that.

'You want to look him over, don't you?'

'No more than he wants to look me over. I'm curious, that's all. But I do mean it about needing the work.'

★ ★ ★

It is pouring with rain as I drive to Harry's. It is a thoroughly miserable morning and for some reason I feel very sad. So why do I feel sad when I was so happy yesterday? It could be the weather, I suppose, or my hormones, or maybe it's got something to do with my parents and those faggots in gravy. I know I keep thinking about it, but I can't make any sense of my thoughts.

When I pass the turn-off to my old home, I try and picture Jack there, talking to Michael about estimates, while they are looking each other over.

Harry is in very good form. I can sense this the moment I let myself into his house. There is an extra cheerfulness about the kitchen which lifts my own spirits marginally.

Coffee is ready on the table. It is in a china coffee jug with pink roses on it, the same pattern as Josephine Brown's teacups, I realise.

I have not written to her since my visit, and she has not written to me. I am not surprised she has not written to me. I left her with little doubt about my opinion of her when she told me, blithely, without concern for my feelings, that I was the result of rape. I must have said something pretty awful because I can still see her horrified expression as I left. It is the only good thing I took away with me from Solihull that day.

We sit across the table from one another. Harry looking pleased with himself, and me curious as to why he is looking so pleased with himself.

Then, without speaking, he takes out a letter from his inside jacket pocket and hands it to me.

I don't ask him what it is, I just look for myself, as Harry expects me to. It is from the publisher we sent his book to.

When I've finished reading the letter, I look up at Harry. Why is he looking so pleased about a rejection?

'It's very encouraging, don't you think, Anna? They say my book is a 'valuable social document' I like that.'

And I like Harry's optimism. He is from the *half full* school of thinking, while I belong to the *half empty* brigade. But optimism is contagious. I read the letter again.

'They even suggest a publisher whose list it might better suit.' I look at Harry, see him beaming, and wish I was more like him.

'That's brilliant, Harry. We'll get it off straight away.'

I decide not to tell him about my change of heart regarding the antiques business idea.

* * *

Jack's just arrived, and we're going out in his van. He rang me an hour ago, and when I said I was feeling a bit low, despite all the excitement about Harry's book, he suggested we went to a folk club. He thinks I need cheering up a bit, and he's probably right, but I don't see how folk music is supposed to help.

All the way there, I try to resist asking him about his meeting with Michael, but as we draw up in the car-park of the pub, I can resist it no longer.

'So?' I say. 'Are you going to be working in my old house, or not?'

Jack gives me a sideways grin, which I find annoying. 'I was beginning to think you weren't interested,' he says.

'I'm not, not really.'

'Liar.'

'Okay, I'm a liar. So what happened then?'

He turns off the engine. 'Not much. He showed me around, told me what he wanted, said he'd have a copy of the plans sent to me.'

'So you're in with a chance, then?' Suddenly I hate the idea of Jack in my old house, chatting away with Michael and Shelly.

'Depends on my estimate.'

'What did you think of the house?'

'Great. It's a beautiful place.' He's looking

directly at me now. 'And if you want to know what I thought of Michael, I thought he was probably a bit of a control freak, but a fairly charming one. He was pleasant enough to me, anyway.'

I don't say anything to this. I want to say that I don't want him going to work there, but I can't bring myself to say it. I want Jack to see it himself without me having to tell him.

But he doesn't say anything so I open the van door and get out.

The back room of the pub is smoky and hot. There are a lot of bearded, middle-aged men drinking pints of beer in straight-sided glasses, and wearing thick, hand-knitted woolly sweaters and sandals without any socks. There are also a lot of middle-aged women with bare, unshaven legs, who've let their hair go grey, drinking orange juice. I assume they have been assigned to driving duty by their beer-drinking partners. I feel out of place and would prefer to go home. But I'm too late to stop Jack paying our three pounds entrance fee.

I find I am in a stroppy mood, and I annoy Jack by insisting on drinking coffee. This means he has to go off to some other part of the pub to get it. So while he's away I find a place at the back of this hot, smoky back room and sit down. I will give it half an hour, I decide.

It is just as bad as I've made up my mind it would be.

Lots of bearded men get up in turn to sing dirgey songs about workhouses and ship-life and being forced to leave their homes and families behind. It is really depressing, and the worst bit is that most people are joining in the chorus lines. I look at Jack and am relieved to see that he isn't.

I let my coffee go cold then drink it in one go. Half an hour must have passed by now, I am thinking. I look at Jack to give him a signal, but he puts up his hand and points at a young man who is getting up and moving to the centre of the room.

'You'll like him,' Jack says.

Disgruntled, I slump back into my seat and study the young man. He is wearing a black tee-shirt and has short hair with a few long thin braids which flick around his shoulders as he moves.

He is getting an accordion out of a leather case. I recognise it because my father had an accordion which he never played. It had belonged to *his* father, apparently, and was kept purely as a memento. I don't have any idea what became of that accordion after my parents died, though I expect I gave it to a charity shop.

The young man starts playing his accordion and I find myself not thinking about anything else but the sound coming from it, and the lyrics of the song he is singing. It is about a young woman who is getting ready for her first dance, and I find it enchanting. Then I realise why. At least I think I know why. It is an Irish folk song, and although I know I have never heard it before, I remember my father singing other songs like this one while he was in the garden. I'd forgotten that my father used to sing to himself, or was he singing to his potatoes?

When the song comes to an end I look at Jack and see he is smiling at me. He takes my hand and I let him keep it.

'This is rather an elaborate lead up to a suggestion that we take a trip to Ireland.'

I'm frowning, wondering what on earth he's on about. But then the young man starts singing again and I can't hear what Jack is saying to me. I have to wait till one of the bearded, middle-aged men, whose straight-sided glass is empty, announces a beer and orange juice break, before I hear the rest.

'I've been worried about you,' Jack's saying. 'You've changed since you went to see your mother.'

'I don't know what you mean.'

'Well, there's the business plan for a start.

You were so keen about it before.'

I look at him, amazed. 'But it was you who talked me out of it.'

'No, Anna, I gave you my opinion. I told you the pitfalls of starting a business, but what I expected was an argument, I expected to thrash things out with you, so you knew what you were getting into. But then I thought you'd go through with it anyway.'

I pull my hand away from him. 'What are you saying exactly?'

'I'm saying that I don't want to be another Michael. I don't want to control your life. And lately I get the feeling that's what you'd like me to do.'

God, I feel angry. This is just so unfair. 'Is that why you didn't answer me when I suggested that you move in with me? Because you think I'm some sort of . . . ' I can't think of the right word — if there is a right word for someone who needs to be controlled.

'I just think you're insecure right now, and you may be making decisions for the wrong reasons.'

I think about my decision to marry Michael after my parents died, but I hate people playing amateur psychologist on me, so I tell him so.

But he doesn't take any notice. 'And you're insecure, I suspect, because you're uncertain about whether or not Josephine Brown is a liar. I'm pretty sure that she is, but the only way you'll know is if you go to Ireland and find out the truth for yourself.'

I look up and see another middle-aged, bearded man getting ready to sing another dirgey song, and I tell Jack that's it, it's time to go.

Nice Young Men and
Steel Magnolias

Michael is standing on my doorstep. It is 2 December, and the morning is cold but sunny. The dogs greet him with half-hearted waggy tails but they soon get fed up with his lack of response and move back into the kitchen, where it's warm.

I have not yet washed, or brushed my hair and must look a terrible mess. I shouldn't mind him seeing me like this, but apparently I do.

He doesn't look all that good himself, come to think of it. His face is still crumpled on one side, from his pillow. I know this means that he's had a bad night. He always lies on his side when he can't sleep. The creases used to drop out quite quickly but his skin is clearly not as resilient as it used to be. I feel no sympathy for him whatsoever.

'I suppose you want to come in,' I say coolly, turning from him.

He follows me and closes the door behind him.

I tell him to go into the kitchen and pour

himself a coffee, if he wants it. Then I nip up the stairs and splash water over my face and put a brush through my hair. I glance at my poster of a sunny lemon grove and it makes me feel better. I would love to live near a lemon grove, to get the benefit of the real thing every day. I would love to live next to a lemon grove in the same way I would love to win the National Lottery jackpot. It is an idle dream without any real expectation of fulfilment.

I put on a quick coat of lipstick and fluff up my hair — almost, but not quite, my *just got out of bed* look — then narrow my eyes to give me a gauzed effect in the bathroom mirror. Then I am mad with myself. Blow this for a lark, he can take me as I bloody well am.

He is sitting by the Rayburn with his coffee. The dogs are lying by his feet, awake but sleepy.

His summer dieting has clearly paid off, as I can see he has lost weight, only it doesn't suit him very much; it makes him look sort of weedy. He is dressed this morning entirely by Pringle, so I assume he has made the detour to my home on his way to the golf course.

'Well?' I say, 'what can I do for you?'

'Did um . . . Jack tell you I'd invited him to tender for the work I'm having done?'

'Yes, um . . . *Jack* did,' I confirm.

'Did he tell you we met?'

I pour myself more coffee. 'Of course he bloody told me, Michael. Why the hell wouldn't he?' I don't sit down because that would make it too cosy. So I press my bottom against one of the work surfaces and wait for his response. The dogs are alert now, disturbed by the tone of my voice.

Michael looks as startled as they do.

'Okay,' he says, 'I only asked. There's no need to jump down my throat.'

He puts his thin, mean lips to the mug and swishes coffee around his teeth. It is a disgusting habit. I always hated it when we were married and I feel pleased I don't have to put up with it now. Poor Shelly.

'I thought he was a very nice young man,' Michael is saying, and succeeds in annoying me more because of the *young* bit.

'That's funny, because I thought Shelly was a very pleasant *young* woman as well.'

He is immune to irony and takes my words at face value. He looks pleased.

So I ask when the Big Day is, blatantly sarcastic now.

He doesn't respond, though. He is looking around the kitchen, seeing if there's anything left worth taking, I would imagine. So I don't have to look at him eyeing my things, I turn away from him and start rinsing my breakfast dishes in the sink.

'I got the impression he's really quite fond of you,' Michael is telling my back.

I turn and face him. 'You sound surprised about that.'

'Of course I'm not,' he protests. 'You're still a fairly attractive woman . . . '

'For my age,' I finish his sentence for him. 'Which is very generous of you, I'm sure, but I can't believe you've just stopped by to wish me well, so why have you really come?'

He shrugs. 'It's the engraving. You said I could have it, so I've come to pick it up.'

I almost laugh, almost but not quite. Instead I shout, I mean really let rip, the sort of letting rip which involves quite a few 'F' words. And as I'm shouting and swearing, Michael just sits there looking vaguely pleased with himself, as if he's happy that he still has the power to make me so mad, which brings me up short and makes me stop shouting.

He gets up from his chair. 'I'll take that as a no then, shall I?'

I almost pick up the nearest blunt object, but when I look at the dogs, who are restless, upset by all the noise I've been making, I decide against it.

Michael walks to the door which leads into my hall, turns, looks at me, and his expression is smug. 'Have you ever considered getting some help for that temper of yours, Anna?'

*　*　*

It's Monday now and Harry and I have just had the long-ago promised lunch together. We ate in Leodis, one of Leeds' fanciest restaurants, and behaved like a couple of toffs. Since his operation, Harry has been a bit more careful about what he eats, but today he left caution at home. And so we went a bit mad, tucked into steak and kidney pie with tons of vegetables, followed by lashings of bread and butter pudding, and washed it all down with regular, calorie-filled Coke. And while we were stuffing ourselves, we astounded each other with our wittiness. We gossiped, we laughed, and not once did we speak of anything remotely serious. To round off a perfect couple of hours, we ordered a single glass of house champagne and toasted Harry's future success. And when we got up from the table we decided we could not possibly eat again for a fortnight.

The mood changed the moment we snapped on our car seat belts. It was that tangible. One minute we were like a couple of drunks on a bender, the next we had entered the maudlin stage.

'We're very alike, you and me, Anna,' Harry says suddenly.

I glance over at him as I drive, surprised and curious.

'Scratch the surface, and beneath is a rich vein of melancholy.'

I think about this. He might be describing me very well but I find it hard to think of Harry this way.

'I can guess what you're thinking, Anna, but I think the only difference is that my surface has just crusted with age, it's harder to scratch.'

We don't speak for a while, but then, when we are reaching the outskirts of the city, Harry brings up the subject of Josephine Brown, and I tell him about Jack's idea to visit Ireland.

Harry thinks it is a good idea.

'I'm glad you confided in me,' he says. 'It's made it a bit easier for me to tell you something about myself.'

I glance his way, surprised as much by his grim tone as his words. I don't know the name of the area we are driving through, but I don't like it very much. It's grey here, and litter-strewn, and has a closed-in feel to it. And it's here where the traffic is usually bad. It is bad today. We are in a long line of stationary traffic now next to *Kwik Fit Autocare*, and for some reason I feel a bit anxious.

I don't reply and he doesn't say anything else for a while. Then: 'Has it ever occurred to you why I don't have any children, Anna?'

'Not especially,' I reply, and it hasn't. 'Though I've always thought you would have made a wonderful father.'

He makes a small rueful sound at this. 'Maybe,' he says, 'but I didn't make a very good husband.'

This, I find hard to believe. Impossible, even. I knew Harry had been married, of course, that his wife died before he moved to the home he has lived in for the past fifty years, but he'd never told me that much about her. I've just always thought her a lucky woman, except for the fact that she died so young.

I glance to my right and note that we have only moved on as far as the Yorkshire TV building.

'I find that very hard to believe, Harry.'

'I wish you could have known Grace, Anna. She was a bit like you in some ways, to look at, that is.'

I am flattered by this and I turn to smile at him, but he doesn't notice. His eyes are fixed on the car ahead of us.

'What sort of person was she?' I ask.

'A typical farmer's daughter in many ways. A good cook, an excellent house-keeper, and when we first started courting there was a lot of fun in her. She used to like to dance; she was a very good dancer, in fact, and I could never quite keep up with her on that score.'

The traffic lights change ahead of us and we move on another few yards.

'You married young,' I say.

'We were both in our early twenties, and the idea was to have children straight away. Grace wanted five. I have no idea why she chose that number.'

He pauses, looks out of the side window now. I look where he's looking and see a group of four grubby, dejected people standing at a bus stop. Maybe they're not grubby or dejected at all, but just seem that way in these grim surroundings.

'But it wasn't going to be as easy as that,' Harry begins again. 'I don't know whose fault it was — if fault be the right word — there weren't any tests in those days.'

This isn't like Harry at all. His stories are usually so wry and amusing, even the sad ones.

'When she started acting a bit odd, the doctor said it was her 'nerves'. That's the best

226

they could come up with then. Any problems in women with no physical cause, were put down to *bad nerves*. He assured me she'd get better in her own good time.'

We are stationary again, two cars back from the traffic lights, which have been holding us up. Ahead, is a Shell petrol station and my eyes are drawn to the bright red and yellow shell motif, lit up from behind. I am beginning to feel distinctly uneasy about this story, and as we move off again, I start counting the arches of a bridge which stretches over the road . . . three, four, five — and then we are under it.

'Only she didn't get better. What she needed was some kind of treatment, but the only thing available was admission to a mental hospital, and I couldn't have allowed that to happen. They were terrible places in those days.'

'I'm sorry, Harry,' I say, 'it must have been awful.'

He sighs deeply. 'It *was* awful to see someone you love in so much pain and anguish and not be able to do anything for them.'

'But you did do something. You looked after her.'

He glances my way. 'But grudgingly, Anna. Not at first, but as the years went on and life

227

became increasingly cheerless, I stopped thinking of Grace and began to think of myself. By the time I reached my late twenties, I'd had enough,' my lovely, caring, patient Harry is telling me.

I look over at Harry's age-spotted hands resting on his lap and I want to reach out and touch them, but I can't bring myself to do it.

'So I looked for diversions.'

Look, Harry, I want to say, look at the silly name of that hairdressers — Steel Magnolias. Wasn't that the name of a film?

'I began an affair.'

And look at that huge white ball on the side of the road. Golf Superstore. Not very subtle, is it? For God's sake, Harry, shut up.

'Only it was more than that, or it seemed it was then, and I seriously considered leaving Grace, but she was in no state to be left. So I stayed, martyring myself. That's how it felt at the time, anyway.'

I don't want to hear any more of this. If I wasn't driving a car now, I would stand up and walk away.

'Then she got worse. She started hurting herself, so of course there was no question of leaving her then.'

The traffic is beginning to flow a bit faster and I take in the names of the pubs that we pass — The Rising Sun, The Cardigan Arms, but it doesn't shut Harry's voice out.

'But I wanted to leave, Anna, I really wanted to.'

There is a long pause now and I want to tell Harry, 'That's it. No more.' But then I think that maybe it will get better, that he will redeem himself, pluck out a happy ending to this terrible story from somewhere.

'I'd employed a young woman to take care of her when I wasn't around, but one day, when the young woman's back was turned, Grace left the house, walked to the nearest railway line and threw herself under a train.'

Iceland Superstore, Netto, The Yorkshire Bank . . .

'I gave up the woman I thought I loved, to punish myself, I suppose. I sold my home, moved to the house I live in now, and began a new life.'

William Hill, The Sandwich Shop, Grime Busters Valeting Service . . .

I can feel him looking at me.

'Anna?'

God, I wish he'd leave me alone.

'Anna, are you all right?'

'Would you do me a favour?' I ask him coldly.

'Of course.'

'Would you please be quiet and let me concentrate on driving.'

* * *

I've decided to bring my plans forward. The plans Jack and I made about going to Ireland. Jack suggested that we went in the spring, next year, but I need to go now or I think I'll go mad. As mad as I was when I was trying to kill Michael.

I think Harry's revelation is the biggest disappointment of my life so far. A far bigger disappointment than Josephine Brown. When I dropped him off at his picture-book house, I sobbed all the way home. I thought he was perfect. And now I know that he isn't, far from it, in fact. He is an adulterous bastard, no better than Michael. And I hate him for disillusioning me. How could he do that to me?

How could he do that to poor Grace?

So I rang the Travel Agents first thing this morning, and I was lucky. There is a special deal on flights from Yeadon to Belfast, so I booked one, using my credit card.

I'm going to get rid of it as soon as I get back from Ireland, so that I can control my finances better.

Jack has just arrived and I will soon have to tell him that I'm going away tomorrow, without him.

He told me yesterday that Michael has offered him the job doing his conversion work — which surprised me considering that last exchange between Michael and me — but that he turned Michael down, which is what I wanted him to do and I should be pleased about it, but I'm too weary to be pleased about anything.

I didn't tell Jack about Michael's visit. There didn't seem any point. I haven't told Jack about Harry, either. I can't break his confidence, no matter how disappointed I am with him.

The dogs are pleased to see Jack. He is good with dogs. He genuinely likes them. And Judd especially likes him. He follows him around the house with a wagging tail. Judd is a man's dog.

I've just made coffee and we drink it silently for a while. He knows I have something to tell him and is waiting for me to begin.

'I'm going to Ireland tomorrow,' I say, when the moment seems right. 'Would you look after the dogs for me while I'm away?'

At first he looks surprised and then, to my surprise, his expression changes and I get the impression that he's not very pleased.

'But I thought it was settled,' he says, 'I thought we were going together.'

'And I thought you said you didn't want to control my life, so this is me being independent.'

Which seems to catch him off guard. I can see him struggling for a good argument, but how can he argue with that?

So he sighs, puts down his cup. 'Fine, you must do what you feel is right. How long will you be away?'

I shrug. 'Not sure, a few days, perhaps, however long it takes.'

He gets up, heads for the door, which annoys me a bit because I want him to stay and help me plan things. 'Do you want me to take the dogs to my place, or will you leave me a key?' He sounds like a neighbour who has grudgingly agreed to do me a favour.

'I can get Nell to do it,' I say, sounding as cool as he did.

'That's up to you, but it will be a long way for her to come twice a day.'

He's right, so I get up and give him a spare set of keys. But I turn my head away when he tries to kiss my cheek.

Toshiba Televisions and Long Lost Fathers

I am staying in a guesthouse in a fairly ordinary, medium sized village, with two shops and four pubs, in the very south of South Armagh. It borders with County Louth in Eire. I like the name, Eire. I can probably see Eire from my bedroom window, which I find strangely exciting.

My room is warm and cosy and very pink, and I am lucky to have found somewhere as nice as this at this time of year. Most guesthouses are closed for winter. I could have stayed in a hotel, I suppose, but that would have been expensive, and anyway I prefer being in someone's home. It makes me feel more secure.

I have been here for two days now. I hired a red Ford Fiesta at Belfast Airport when I arrived and drove south, with only a vague idea of where I was heading. I'm not an organised traveller, which is why I could have done with Jack's help, but so far I have managed quite well on my own. How I came to be here, in my father's village, is a matter of chance. I didn't set out to come here. I only came here at all because I saw a sign for Killiough on a main road and remembered the name. I feel a bit sad that he never brought me here when I was young. But then, my father was not a sentimental man and as his relatives were all dead or in England, I assume he simply saw no reason to come here again. Since he had little to say for himself, I have to make many assumptions about my father.

Yesterday was cold but sunny, so I wrapped myself up in my woollies and borrowed a bike from the woman who runs the guesthouse. I spent the day crossing to and fro over the border, as my father might have done when he was a boy. It is a gently rolling landscape, with high banked hedges lining the roadsides. It is not so picturesque as my part of Yorkshire, and most of the houses I came upon were not quaint, stonebuilt cottages, but characterless bungalows with huge, untended gardens. I dare say it will have changed a lot since my father was last here, forty-odd years ago. I know it has, because my landlady told me that the house my father's family lived in was pulled down a long time ago to make way for one of those characterless bungalows. She didn't know very much else about his family, they weren't famous for anything, no local myths or legends had grown up about them, but I did find a few graves with the same surname as my father's in the churchyard.

I kept expecting to see road blocks and soldiers with submachine guns around every bend, but in fact I have seen very little military presence. No doubt the current cease-fire has a lot to do with that. My landlady assures me that this one will last, but perhaps that is just wishful thinking.

Until now, I feel as if I have been on holiday. I have been quietly enjoying myself, getting to know my dad a bit, and I have been in no hurry to do what I came here to do. Or perhaps I have just been putting it off.

I *have* been putting it off, if I'm honest. But I can put it off no longer. Today I must get down to business. Today I must set about looking for what I came here to find.

All that I know so far, is that Killiough is about five miles from the house Josephine Brown grew up in. I know this because of my birth certificate. It came into my possession when my mother died. Until then, I had not seen it since that day when I was eight, when I found it in the scratched biscuit tin with the Houses of Parliament on the lid.

My parents never did tell me that I was adopted. They may have been misguided in withholding such important information from me, but I expect their intentions were good: I suspect they thought that it would unsettle me. I don't think it occurred to them that I would need my birth certificate when I got married, any more than it occurred to them that I would get my hands on it when they died. I have often wondered how I would have felt had I only learned the truth then.

I do not know the actual address of Josephine Brown's former home. Only the area is mentioned on the certificate. But the area is fairly small, a scattering of houses over the lower, western slopes of a mountain with the romantic-sounding name of Slieve Gullion. It means simply, *Mountain of the Steep Slope*. I looked it up in the guide book I bought at the airport. It is the highest mountain in County Armagh, and I can see it in the distance from the dining-room window of the guesthouse.

★   ★   ★

I set out in my hired Ford Fiesta and drive towards the mountain. The landscape as I approach it is very dramatic. It is surprising how much it has changed in a mere five miles. There are low clouds looming over the mountain and a mist is gathering, which adds to the drama of the rocky landscape, and probably means that it is soon going to rain.

I know from my map that I am in the area I am looking for, though there are no road signs or landmarks to confirm this. So I stop at the first house I come to and get out of the car. It is a characterless bungalow. A bungalow with a long winding drive and two outrageous rampant lions on whitewashed gate posts.

A young woman answers the door. She has a very freckled face and she looks extremely harassed. I tell her I am looking for the former home of the Brady family. That I understand the Bradys used to live around here. I realise as I am saying all this that I am lacking a plan. Finding where my mother came from is one thing, finding information is quite a different matter. But I have to start somewhere, I suppose.

The young woman looks at me blankly then shakes her head. 'No Bradys round here now,' she says.

She starts closing the door then opens it wide again. 'You could try Mrs Roach, down the road. She's been here for years and knows everyone. You can't miss it. Just look out for a red roof.'

* * *

The red roof is corrugated metal of some kind. The door of the single-storey dwelling is also painted red, and the walls of the house are washed in lime. It is one of the few old buildings I have come across.

An old woman answers when I knock on the red door. She looks how I would expect an old woman who lives in a house like this to look. All that is missing is a black shawl.

She regards me with some suspicion when I use her name and tell her I am trying to find the house in which a Josephine Brady grew up. When I add that I am a relative of the said Josephine Brady, her manner becomes even more reserved. I sense that she knows who I am talking about, and I am amazed that it has been so easy. Except it isn't going to be as easy as all that because she is closing the door on me. I turn and start walking down the path, back to my car, not knowing what to make of such a reaction.

Then perhaps she feels sorry for me, because just as I am fumbling with my key in the car lock, she calls out to me.

'You'd better come inside,' she says, though it sounds more like an order.

When I am inside, she asks if I would like tea, but I don't like to put her to the trouble. The room smells of something unpleasant, something familiar but which I can't quite put my finger on. The windows are very small and the room is dark and oppressive. I hate dark rooms and I am itching to put a light on.

The old woman ignores my refusal of tea and switches on an electric kettle. It looks very out of place in this room, which has an ancient range and patterned lino and a scrub-top table, so scrubbed it has turned the wood white. In the corner of the room is another sore thumb: a large-screen Toshiba television. The TV is on but the sound is turned down. The surreal quality of my current situation is heightened by 'This Morning's' Richard and Judy silently mouthing pleasantries to one another.

The woman has me sit down close to the range, on a chair covered with a gaudily crocheted blanket. She seems to be all courtesy now and willingness to please.

'There,' she says, when I am seated, 'let me look at you, now.'

How she can see me in this dim light defeats me. She must have some sort of super-vision. She is looking me over so closely I should feel uncomfortable, but she is doing it in a manner that, like a gynaecologist making an intimate examination, seems too professionally distanced to cause serious embarrassment.

'Mmm,' she murmurs, turning from me to

239

pour water into a stainless steel teapot, 'I think I can see a likeness.'

This, of course, is nonsense. I don't look remotely like Josephine Brown, or Brady, but perhaps she is just being pleasant, or perhaps she is just old and forgetful. Or perhaps she hasn't a clue who Josephine Brady is and is just lonely and in need of some company.

I watch her as she clatters cups and saucers on the scrub-top table. She is small and stout. Her cheeks are healthily pink, and she looks the sort of woman who will live well into her nineties. For all I know, she might already be into her nineties.

'This is very kind of you, Mrs Roach,' I say. 'My name is Anna, by the way.'

'I wondered what name she'd given you.'

I take the plain white cup and saucer from her. The tea in it is orange-coloured, very strong.

'So?' she says, sitting down on an upright chair at the table, so she is looking down on me.

I imagine 'So?' is an invitation to explain myself. But how much should I tell her? Does it matter if I am honest? I decide that it doesn't. In all probability I will never see Mrs Roach again, so why should I worry what she thinks of me?

'I recently met up with Josephine Brady in

England, and she told me something which has left me unsettled. Did you know her when she was young?'

She is looking at me through narrowed eyes, trying to make sense of my rambling, I expect.

'I did, aye.'

'Did she live far from here?'

'She lived a half-mile away. It would have been the next house you came to on this road. Only there's not much of it left now.'

'No one lives there now, then?'

'They'd have a job on,' Mrs Roach says with a shrug, 'the roof caved in years ago. And no wonder, the way it has been neglected. Josephine could have had it fixed up after her parents passed on, but she just wanted rid of the place. It's been on sale now for years, only nobody wants it. Nowadays I'd say, it's no more than a liability.'

'Josephine was the only child, then?'

'Aye, and spoilt rotten, she was. She broke her poor mother's heart, she did. Never once came back to see her after she went away to England.'

It is obvious that Mrs Roach doesn't like Josephine Brady very much, which is fine by me, and it does seem to suggest that we really are speaking about the same unlikeable person.

241

'Did everyone know when she became pregnant with me?'

She seems to think this a silly question. 'Of course we knew, despite all the pretence of her going away to stay with an aunty. That's what they all said when a girl went away to have her baby. Ah, we went along with it, of course, but we all knew the truth.'

I have managed to drink most of my tea. It would be rude to leave it. I just hope she doesn't insist on topping my cup up. I'm not all that sure that I care for Mrs Roach very much, she is just a bit smug and opinionated for my liking.

I hesitate before asking my next question. By now I am certain that she will know the answer, but I am afraid of having my fears confirmed. But I have come to find out, so I glance at Richard and Judy for support. They are interviewing a well known soap star from 'Brookside'.

'Did anyone know how she came to be pregnant with me?'

Mrs Roach puts down her cup and looks at me with surprise. Then she lets out a loud cackling laugh.

'The same way we all get pregnant, I shouldn't wonder,' she says when she recovers a bit, then cackles some more at her own wittiness. Her sturdy body is rocking

242

over the table as she cackles.

I am not in the least offended by this outburst. It has given me hope.

'Is it known who fathered the child?' I find myself deliberately distancing myself from the situation to encourage frankness. I do not think Mrs Roach is a sensitive woman but she may have depths I am not so far aware of.

'Didn't I tell you there was a likeness when you came in here?' she answers cryptically. 'I had to look hard, but I can see Danny Madden in you, all right.'

Danny who? I am thinking. *Madden* sounds like mad — the sort of name a rapist might very well have.

'Danny Madden?' I repeat.

'Aye, Danny Madden. Only he's not Danny any more, of course. He's Daniel now. Daniel Madden.'

Richard and Judy and the star from 'Brookside' are laughing about something.

'Who is Daniel Madden?' I ask.

'Why, he's your father, of course. Who else would he be?'

I can feel my heart thumping.

'Is he a rapist?' I say.

Mrs Roach is staring at me.

'Is he a What? Be God, where did you get an idea like that from now?' She is cackling again, then the cackling stops and she becomes deadly serious. 'Did she tell you that, that little missen?'

I find it hard to think of Josephine Brown as a Little Missen.

'She didn't say who raped her, just that she was raped.'

'Well then, she's a liar, and a bare-faced one at that,' Mrs Roach says, and she does not look at all pleased. I think she is angry with me, and I wonder if I should leave.

But I can't leave now, so I shall risk making her angrier still.

'Can you tell me about Daniel Madden?' I ask.

She is looking at me as she did when I was standing on her doorstep, suspicious again.

'I can tell you he wouldn't take kindly to being accused of r . . . ' She tries to use the word, but it gets stuck in her throat. ' . . . the thing you are accusing him of.'

'I'm not accusing him of anything,' I protest. 'I'm only repeating what I've been told.'

'Well, I'm not sure you should go round repeating that kind of thing. It could get you into a lot of trouble, young woman.' Then she stands up and takes my cup from me. It is a dismissive gesture I think I would be foolish to disregard. So I get up and make for the door.

'Thank you for the tea,' I say, remembering my manners, though I am numb to all other feeling. 'I'm sorry to have upset you. It really wasn't my intention.'

She doesn't reply so I open the door and step outside. It has just started raining.

Mrs Roach lets out a big sigh. 'Will you look at that weather now, and my washing out on the line.'

I give her a sympathetic look, which is the best I can manage.

'I'll tell you what,' she says, her expression that of a street tradesman about to make me an offer I can't possibly refuse. 'Get the washing in for me now, and I'll tell you all about Danny Madden.'

I hesitate. But only for a moment.

Dry Coffee Cake and Christmas Shopping

I flew back to England first thing this morning. I feel as if I have been away for ages, far more than three days, and yet I am in no hurry to get home.

I had the taxi driver drop me in Ilkley, and I am taking my time over a pot of Darjeeling in the tearoom. I am looking forward to seeing the dogs, but not people. I don't know why I am feeling this way. I should be pleased with the knowledge that I was not after all violently conceived. That the man who was my father — who provided the necessary sperm for my conception — isn't a rapist, but just an ordinary sort of man living a quiet and comfortable life in Dublin, recently retired from his work as a city GP.

According to Mrs Roach, anyway.

When I heard all this, I seriously thought about going to see him, getting straight in my hired Ford Fiesta and driving to Dublin. But then I thought better of that idea and went to look at the house with the caved in roof, that had been the childhood home of Josephine

Brady. It was a bleak and depressing sight, and since then I've been like I am now, sort of flat and miserable, which isn't at all how I'm supposed to be.

I am beginning to think it is not in my nature to be happy, not for long, anyway. I should be counting my blessings right now, but I can't think of any so maybe I'm more like my mother than I thought I was.

I look about me, admire the large collection of interesting teapots displayed around the tearoom, listen to the buzz of pleasant chatter, and wonder how it is that everyone can be so cheerful.

In an attempt to cheer up my own life, I order more tea and some coffee cake, only when it arrives the cake is dry and not very coffeeish and I don't feel cheered up at all. So I just drink my tea and make myself more miserable by thinking about Harry and how much he's let me down, about Michael and what a shit he was, about Jack and how cold he was last time I saw him — and I realise it is true. I am my mother all over again. A real chip off the old block.

Just when I think I have exhausted all the bad things in my life, I glance up and see my worst nightmare approaching, a spectacle in shocking pink and black patent stilettos.

'Anna! Where on earth have you been?'

Hilary calls out, so loud everyone in the tearoom looks at her, then at me. 'I've been trying to get hold of you for ages.' She is looking at my holdall which is taking up a chair next to mine.

I don't think she has any right to know where I've been so I shrug. 'Just away,' I tell her. I'm hoping to put her off sitting down at my table by refusing her eye contact, but I'd forgotten about her immunity to body language, so she sits down anyway.

'Have you heard the news?' she wants to know and she sounds oddly desperate, as if she's hoping I haven't.

I'd like to tell her what to do with herself, as usual, but it seems I am too polite, or too weary.

'What news is that, Hilary?' I ask, without interest.

'About Shelly?'

'What about Shelly?'

She lets out a sigh of relief. She is thrilled that she is going to be the one to tell me whatever it is she knows.

'It's awfully sad,' she says, sounding remarkably cheerful. The waitress comes to take her order and she brushes her rudely away. 'I haven't had time to look at the menu, yet,' she snaps, though she always has lemon tea and a crumpet.

'Poor dear,' she goes on, as the waitress moves away from the table, 'she was taken into hospital two days ago. Michael is devastated, of course. They both are.'

I have no idea what she is talking about. Maybe I haven't been listening properly.

'It's so sad,' she repeats. 'I mean, she must have been over four months into the pregnancy by now.'

I begin to catch on. 'Are you saying Shelly has miscarried the baby?'

Hilary is looking at me as if I am stupid. 'Well, obviously, Anna, what else could I mean?'

I look at Hilary, see the pleasure in her face at someone else's misfortune, and I want to punch her. But I manage to control myself. So instead of punching her, I say:

'I think it's time I told you something, Hilary.' I can feel myself trembling, I'm not sure why, though I expect it is due to the rage I am feeling.

She doesn't answer, but she is on her guard.

I get up and consider pouring milk over her recently highlighted hair, but once again, resist temptation.

'I think you should know, that you are the most contemptible, unfeeling cow I have ever had the misfortune to know.'

Then I grab my holdall and move away from the table before I say something I might actually regret.

'But Anna,' she says to my back, her voice an irritating whine, 'I thought you'd be pleased.'

* * *

What's really awful is that I might be. Pleased, I mean. I'm not pleased that a baby has died, of course, or a foetus, as I suppose it was not technically a baby yet. Of course I'm not pleased about that.

But is that really true?

Of course it is. What sort of person would I be if I was pleased?

I would be a monster.

Perhaps I am a monster, because if I am really honest, part of me is very pleased indeed.

So I ring Nell to see if it's okay to feel like this. I don't think I can decide for myself.

'You must have very mixed feelings about the news,' Nell says, before I get a chance to tell her how confused I am.

'Bless you, Nell. I'm glad you said that. You don't know how glad.'

Since I do not much feel like talking about my trip now, she asks if she can call over tomorrow. I tell her that I'd love to see her. I say it, but I'm not at all sure that I mean it.

★ ★ ★

Jack brought a take-away round because he knew I wouldn't have had the chance to get any shopping in. I think he is trying to make up for being so horrible to me last time I saw him, but I wish he hadn't bothered. I'd sooner have been on my own tonight. I really do feel a bit odd-distracted, remote, I'm not quite sure how to describe it. The strange thing is that I seem to be functioning fairly normally, doing what has to be done, but it's as if I'm not really in charge.

Maybe Michael's right. Maybe I do need help of some kind, not for my temper, which only he brings out, but with the rest of it. Maybe I need to talk to somebody who isn't involved, who can be objective.

'Maybe you should talk to someone,' Jack says when I have been staring into the fire for about half an hour.

I drag my eyes from the flames and glare at him. 'Are you saying I need psychiatric help?' I demand from my high horse, ignoring the fact that he was echoing my very own thoughts.

'Why do you make it sound as if a

psychiatrist is a bad thing? They're just doctors, who specialise.'

'Yeah!' I get up from my chair and throw my arms about like a drama queen. I know I'm being childish. I can hardly resist stamping my feet. 'A doctor who deals with mad people.'

'Anna! For God's sake.'

He looks so handsome tonight, this man who tells me he loves me. But how could he love me? How could he love someone so much older than he is, who's got wrinkles and the beginnings of jowls, and who, according to him, needs psychiatric help?

'If you won't talk to me you really should speak to someone. You've been through a lot lately — the divorce, meeting your mother, being told she was raped.'

And the rest! I say to myself, thinking of Harry, only I don't want to think of Harry. And I don't say anything to Jack. Which seems to annoy him.

'You're supposed to feel better now, now you know it was all a lie, but you seem worse.' He sounds exasperated. 'And if you won't talk to me, perhaps a professional can help you unravel your feelings. Maybe there's something else which is bothering you. Something you haven't dealt with yet.' He sighs. 'And I don't mean a psychiatrist, anyway. Just a counsellor. Someone who's trained to bring these things out.'

I sit in my chair and look at the fire again. 'I don't need a counsellor,' I tell him. 'Nell's coming over tomorrow, I can talk to her.'

I hear him sigh, and it occurs to me that he's hurt by that remark but I can't really be bothered. I look at the upholstery on the arms of my chair and decide that it needs re-covering.

'Did I tell you that Shelly lost her baby?' I hear myself saying.

Jack does not reply straight away, and because I can't take my eyes off the fading, threadbare upholstery, I can't see the expression on his face.

'No,' he says eventually, 'you didn't.'

Maybe I'll go for something completely different next time. Get rid of the chintz, have something a bit more modern. Maybe I'll get rid of all the old stuff, start again, go for a minimalist look. Maybe I'll sell this house and buy a characterless bungalow.

'Is that going to make any difference to their plans to get married?'

I look up from the arm of my chair. I hadn't thought of that.

★ ★ ★

Nell and I are walking alongside the river bank. The dogs are ahead of us sniffing and shuffling about on the water's edge. Rusty loves the water and keeps dropping a stick at my feet in the hope that I will throw it into the river for him to retrieve. But the water's too cold and he is too old.

I'm not quite sure how I feel today. I do know that I would have liked to have stayed in bed, watched the 'EastEnders' omnibus, see what's been happening in Albert Square lately. I would have as well, if Nell hadn't been coming.

'So,' Nell says when I've told her about my meeting with Mrs Roach. 'Danny Madden was a decent young man, after all. Not an evil rapist, as that awful woman would have had you believe.'

'Apparently not. He wanted to marry her, strange fellow. He was prepared to postpone his plans to train as a doctor. He was going to get a job to support all three of us.'

'But Josephine wasn't having any of that?'

'No. She blamed him for ruining her life, which sounds just the sort of thing she would say.'

'Well, Danny Madden sounds all right to me,' Nell says, all smiles.

'I suppose so, if I can believe Mrs Roach, that is.'

'Do you believe her?'

'I want to.'

'Well, why don't you get in touch with him, find out for sure?'

Rusty is being persistent, so I pick up his stick and throw it away from the water. He looks at me as if I have lost my senses but runs after it anyway.

'I've thought about it.' I tell her how I almost drove straight down to Dublin, but changed my mind. 'I just don't think I could take any more disappointments just now, and anyway, if he knows that I exist, which he must, he would have made contact with me if he'd wanted to.'

'Maybe it wasn't that easy for him. Maybe he's tried and failed. Maybe Josephine told him you were dead. I wouldn't put anything past her.'

Rusty has dropped the stick at my feet again.

'Who knows? Whatever, I still think it's best left alone. I'm beginning to think it's a mistake to mess about with the past.' Besides, since being in Killiough, in my dad's village, I would feel even more disloyal if I went off looking for a man I don't even know just because he fertilised the egg which turned out to be me.

We put the dogs on leads as we pass

through a field full of listless sheep.

'It's just struck me,' Nell says. 'How did your parents come to adopt you, anyway? I thought your father was living in England for years before you were born. Your mother was English, wasn't she?'

I nod. 'Yes, and Mrs Roach explained that, too. She was a real fund of information once she got going.'

'And?' says Nell.

'Well, my dad moved to England, married, then I think his father died and he moved back to Killiough with his wife for a bit, to sort things out. So that's when it must have happened.'

'You never talk about them much.'

I shrug. 'There's not much to say.'

We walk in silence for quite a while, then Nell brings up the Michael and Shelly thing, and we talk about that for a bit, and we both end up deciding that we really are sorry for Shelly, but that maybe it's all for the best. Which is rather trite, I suppose, but it's all we could come up with.

It starts to drizzle so we turn around, and as we walk back beside the river, I tell her about my last meeting with Michael, and how he wanted the engraving and how mad I got with him.

'Isn't it about time you stopped getting

mad with him,' she says. 'You should let it go now. Try and move on.'

I look at her, puzzled. 'I don't know what you mean,' I say.

★ ★ ★

I am determined to make everything perfect for Megan's homecoming. I've decided that's what is missing in my life at the moment — a sense of purpose. So I went to the garden centre when Nell went home, and bought lots of holly and mistletoe, which I put in the garden to keep it fresh. It helped a bit, it made me feel like I was making an effort.

I made a great effort this morning and got up really early. I've decided to get my Christmas shopping done in plenty of time for once, and so I drove into Leeds at eight, to make sure of a decent parking space.

I buy Jack's present first, a sweater which he can wear to that horrible folk club if he ever drags me off there again. Then I spend ages in the plush cosmetics section of a department store, being seduced into buying all sorts of things I had no intention of buying before I arrived. I'm convinced that department stores are deliberately contaminated with some little known substance that induces temporary insanity, a madness that makes people spend lots of money against their will.

By midday I am exhausted, weary of crowds and queues, and craving caffeine and carbohydrates.

The department store café is full, so I look for a pub. I find one without too much trouble. It's smart and modern, and looks like the sort of place women can go into alone without raising eyebrows. I adjust my eyes to the dim light and think myself lucky to find a seat. I claim it by leaving my bags on the chair and watch them while I'm at the bar.

I order my coffee, a pot, and a turkey and stuffing sandwich, and when I sit down again I start delving into my bags. I've already forgotten what I've bought, which adds weight to my sinister substance conspiracy theory, I decide. Still, by the look of things Nell and Megan will be pleased.

When my order is delivered to the table I tuck straight in, and while I am eating and drinking I listen to a couple of businessmen at the next table to mine, talking about football. It's boring stuff, but listening to them is better than listening to the goings on in my head. But the things in my head are very persistent, and I find myself switching off from the football and thinking about Harry, and how much I miss him, or rather how much I miss the man that I thought he was.

Then I stop thinking about Harry when I hear a familiar voice. I glance over my shoulder in the direction of the voice, and see Raymond sitting two tables away from mine. Oh God, I think, not Hilary. But I can't hear Hilary's voice, so after a bit I take another quick peak and see that Raymond is in deep conversation with a well-dressed red-head. They are both drinking gin and tonic, by the looks of it, and the red-head is smoking a cigarette. I find I can look at them freely if I adjust myself a little in my seat. Raymond has his back to me and the red-head is at right angles to him so I have her full profile in view.

They are speaking quietly, and I sense from this, and how close their heads are together, that it's not about health insurance. When Raymond takes the woman's free hand in his, I am convinced of this.

I feel embarrassed at being a witness to whatever is going on, and so I knock back my coffee and beat a speedy retreat. I don't even finish all my sandwich.

I should be pleased. I mean, Hilary has been such a bitch to me, but I don't feel pleased at all. I feel incredibly sad.

Surprise Packages and Old Christmas Cards

A brown padded envelope is waiting on my coconut mat this morning. Beside it are a couple of Christmas cards (I really must get round to writing some myself), a bill of some kind, and the usual news that I may have won £50,000.

The padded envelope interests me most, so it is the first thing to receive my attention. I sit down with it at my kitchen table, note that it was posted yesterday, the 11th, and then open it to an audience of two. The dogs are waiting for their breakfast, but at this moment they seem as intrigued as I am by the envelope.

I take out the contents, a small wad of official-looking papers, together with a letter from a firm of solicitors, based in Solihull. I read the letter, and am bewildered by it.

It is a fairly long letter, with a lot of incomprehensible legal jargon, so I read it again and this time just focus on the relevant bits.

. . . Mrs Josephine Brown, née Brady, will shortly be returning to Canada where she intends to take up permanent residence.

. . . I am instructed by my client that she wishes to make a gift to you of a house and a small parcel of land in the Country of Armagh, in Northern Ireland, the details of which are enclosed . . .

I glance at the said enclosed details, and in particular at a photocopied section of an Ordnance Survey map, on which a small area has been ringed in red pen. It is the piece of land on which the Brady house stands, the house whose roof has now caved in.

I look at Rusty. 'What do you think?' I ask him. 'Is this her trying to salve her conscience?'

Rusty doesn't seem to have an opinion, but then Judd tries to get in on the act and pushes his wet nose at my hand, forcing me to pat his head. I think of that house which has been on the market for years, that nobody wants, and I remember what Mrs Roach said about it, and I'm not bewildered any more.

'So the cow is trying to offload her liabilities on to me,' I tell the dogs, and they start wagging their tails, as if they agree with me.

I can't help laughing at the thought. Then I think of her 'ungrateful' children in Canada, whose lives are soon to be blighted by their mother's presence, and I laugh a bit louder.

I don't bother to enclose a covering letter, I just seal up the envelope with sellotape, and readdress it to the sender. Then I feed the dogs, take them for a walk, drop the padded envelope off at the postbox on my way. And I feel good, better than I have for ages.

Only I don't feel quite so good when I get back to the house. In fact, I feel edgy and restless, then I remember about being purposeful, and how much better I feel when I'm doing something, so I go into the junk room and decide to look for some Christmas cards. I am sure I have some left over from last year, when I was living in my lonely flat, and didn't feel like sending cards to anyone. And if I can find them now, I should save myself a couple of quid.

One of these days, I am going to do something with my junk room, but right now it's still full of all the things I didn't know what to do with when I moved into the house. Mainly cardboard boxes, stashed with things I have mostly forgotten about.

The first box I come to is Megan's box, which is large and sturdy, and very distracting. I cannot resist going through it, reminding myself of everything my daughter ever did or achieved. I get a bit sentimental as I look at her things, from a paper rosette for third place in the egg and spoon race, when she was five, right through to her 'A' Level results. Sentimental, and a bit maudlin as well, when I realise how fast it's all gone. Then, right in the middle of feeling sentimental and maudlin, I get a sort of ache inside me, a really physical thing. I can't work out what might be the cause of the ache at first, then I think about Harry and his poems, and I decide that it might have something to do with love and loss and stuff like that. Which makes me wail, a bit like how I imagine a banshee wails, because I realise that I have probably lost my little girl to a young man called Brandon who lives six thousand bloody miles away.

When I'm all wailed out, I wipe my nose on my sleeve, laugh at myself for being such a misery, pack Megan's things away again, and make myself do what I came into the junk room to do in the first place.

I eventually find the Christmas cards in an old fisherman's basket that Michael and I found washed up on a beach somewhere a long time ago. We used to keep logs in it in the early days.

The cards aren't very special, I realise, just

supermarket cheapos, but they'll do. No one really appreciates it if they receive expensive cards anyway. I know I don't. So I stack the boxes away again, close the door on the mess, and get down to writing the cards straight away.

My Christmas card list has reduced considerably this year. All those people who have snubbed me since the divorce have been firmly crossed off, which will cut down on postage.

I decide to make more of a fuss than usual of the people who have been loyal to me. Instead of the usual brief messages, I am writing proper letters with in-depth enquiries about peoples' lives and health, and providing lots of positive information about how brilliantly everything is going for me these days. It's okay for me to feel sorry for myself, but I don't want anyone else feeling sorry for me any more.

I realise that the best part of two hours has gone by when the telephone rings.

'Hello Anna, it's Harry.'

Oh dear, I think, not Harry. I'm just not ready for this yet.

'Hello, Harry. How are you?' I think I sound normal.

'Sorry not to have heard from you lately. I must have upset you badly.'

What am I supposed to say to that? I think about making an excuse for not calling him, but because I am disarmed by his refusal to beat around the proverbial bush, I tell him the truth. 'Yes, Harry. You did. And I wish you hadn't told me.'

'You mean you'd have preferred it if I'd let you carry on believing what a charming old man I was?'

'Yes. I would.'

I hear him sigh. 'Can we talk about this, Anna? I could come over now.'

I feel a bit panicky at the thought of seeing him, so I tell him it isn't possible, that I'm really busy, but maybe sometime. 'Have you heard anything more about the book?' I hear myself asking him, because I can't bear the disappointment in his voice, and because I am still fond of him however hard I've tried not to be.

'Nothing yet, but I remain hopeful. What about Ireland? Nell told me you'd gone but I didn't like to ask her any details. How was it?'

'It was fine. I'll tell you all about it when I see you.'

'I'll look forward to it,' he says, sounding just a bit chirpier now.

I put down the phone and picture poor Grace, alone with her mental illness, while Harry is out with his *fancy woman*. I am sure

Grace would have thought of that other woman this way if she'd known what was going on. And I'd like to bet that she did know.

*   *   *

I keep myself occupied for the rest of the day, forcing myself to do things. The last job I did was to prepare the spare room for Megan and Brandon, and I did it with care, with loads of attention to detail, because I felt guilty for thinking bad things about Brandon.

But then I ran out of things to do, so I opened a bottle of wine. I have three-quarters of it inside me when the door bell rings. I glance at my watch, see that it is only seven-fifteen, and Jack isn't due till eight.

Rusty and Judd are giving meaning to their existence by barking their heads off, a neutral sort of bark, which gives no indication whether the caller is known to them or not.

It turns out to be someone very well known to them, but not at all well known to me. I realise as I open the door to Michael, that twenty-odd years of marriage just wasn't long enough to get to know this particular man. He looks miserable, fed up, depressed, which must mean that he has feelings after all, that he has taken the miscarriage badly.

I lead him into the kitchen and reluctantly offer him what's left in the wine bottle. I'm in the mood for getting drunk and if he accepts I will just fall short of my aim. There is nothing else left in the house to drink.

He accepts, and doesn't even seem to mind that it's cheap Bulgarian.

'I'm sorry to hear what happened,' I say, not certain whether it's the truth or not. 'How is Shelly coping?'

He shrugs, a sort of off-hand shrug, which tells me Shelly's welfare is not uppermost on his mind at the moment.

'She's okay, I suppose.'

He swallows the contents of his glass in one go and I suspect that it's not his first tonight.

He puts the glass down on the table, sits, pats Judd's head. 'Look, Anna,' he says, looking at Judd now as if it is him he is speaking to. 'This thing with Shelly and me, it's not working out.'

'I'm sorry to hear that, Michael.' And I am, as well. I am especially sorry for Shelly, who must be feeling like shit at this moment, alone, having just lost a baby, while the man she lives with is at his ex-wife's house, telling her — telling her what, exactly?

He has stopped patting Judd's head and is looking at me now. 'It's not working out,' he says, 'because I keep thinking about you.'

I feel like laughing, but how can I laugh at such a sick joke.

'Don't you realise how much I've been missing you, Anna? How much this, this thing with that builder chap has hurt me?'

Just for a moment there, I am stunned. Michael, admitting to being hurt by something. It is like learning that Saddam Hussein does work in his spare time for Amnesty International. Only then I catch a certain glint in his eye, a glint which tells me he believes he has caught me off my guard, which he had, but I'm not off guard anymore, and suddenly it's all very clear to me.

'I know why you've really come here,' I say, 'and it's nothing to do with being hurt, or with missing me. You're just up to your old tricks, Michael. You're hoping for a bit of pity and comfort, the sort of comfort you used to seek from other women when we were married.'

He looks a bit taken aback by this, and I find myself smiling. I can't help it. It's so damn amusing, or it would be if it wasn't for Shelly.

'I expect the novelty value quite appeals to you, too. Coming here, to your ex-wife, of all people. And think of the added fun you'd have in knowing the mischief you'd cause between me and Jack. If I was fool enough to fall for it, that is. I wondered why you asked him to do that work on your house, now I'm beginning to see. It must have been quite a blow when he turned you down.'

'And why would I want to cause mischief? This is crazy, Anna.'

'Because that's what you're like,' I tell him without emotion. (Nell, I decide, would be proud of me.) 'You like to pull people's strings, be in control. I see now what a nightmare it must have been for you when I left. Not because you cared about me, but because you lost control of me. That's why you started asking for my things. You didn't really want them, you just enjoyed the sense of power it gave you.'

I turn from him and open one of the cupboards, to see if there is any cooking sherry in there. There isn't.

When I look back at him, I see that the glint in his eye has turned into an angry gleam.

'Now something else has happened which you don't have any control over, so you've decided to see if you can mess up my life again, just to make yourself feel better. Well, it's no go, Michael. Leaving you was the best thing I ever did, and if you think I'd fall for all that old codswallop again, you're well and truly mistaken.'

There is a long silence, then: 'You really are not a well woman, do you know that, Anna? Only a very odd person would see all that in a perfectly innocent remark about missing you.'

'Well, sorry Michael, but I don't think Shelly would think it was very bloody innocent.'

'I hope that isn't a threat,' he says.

'Why should it matter what I tell her? You said it wasn't working out, didn't you?'

He gets up and for a moment I think he's going to hit me, and then . . .

. . . And then the back door opens and Jack walks in. It is not a good moment. The atmosphere in my kitchen must be very tense.

'I'm sorry,' Jack says, looking at me, then at Michael. 'I hope I am not interrupting anything?'

'Of course you're not,' I say, a bit too quickly. 'Michael has just come over to tell me about Shelly's miscarriage. He didn't know we'd already heard about it.' Why I feel it necessary to cover up is a mystery.

Jack looks at Michael again and I can see he's not in the least convinced by my lie.

'We were very sorry to hear about it,' Jack says, taking my hand in his. I can feel the tension in him as he massages my fingers.

'Thanks,' Michael says, or rather mumbles. 'Well, best be on my way, I suppose.'

Jack is quiet when we are alone again. He is looking at the empty bottle of wine and two wine glasses and picturing a scene which did not happen. I think about telling him the truth, what really happened, but all that stuff with Michael has drained me, and I don't feel like talking about it. Not yet, anyway.

And because I think another drink might help, I insist he takes me out to a pub.

We drive quite a long way, to a place I haven't been into before, but it's cosy and festive and we sit by an open fire and while I drink Whisky Mac, because it's Christmassy *and* fairly strong, Jack drinks Coke, because he is driving.

I'm just on the verge of telling Jack what happened with Michael, when I notice how down he seems.

'Is everything okay?' I ask him.

He looks up at me from his Coke.

'Do you really give a damn if things are okay for me, Anna?'

I'm a bit shaken by this, I have to admit. I can't think how to respond.

'Have you any idea what you've been like lately?' He almost sounds cross now; his voice is ever so slightly raised, and I wonder why he is talking to me this way.

'I don't know what you mean,' I answer defensively, and I don't. I know I was a bit strange when I came back from Ireland, but I'm all right now.

He sighs noisily.

'No, Anna, you wouldn't know, would you? That's because you've become so self-centred.' He puts up his hand to stop me interrupting, protesting my innocence.

'I know you've had a hard time. I appreciate that and I've been there for you whenever you needed me. You'll give me that much, I hope.'

'I suppose so,' I concede — grudgingly, because I don't like the way this seems to be going.

'But when are you ever there for me?'

I down my drink for something to do rather than reply to this. I notice out of the corner of my eye that Jack is twisting his glass round and round on the table. He is clearly agitated about something, but his words aren't making very much sense to me.

'When did you last ask me about *my* life?'

This is just so unfair. 'I just asked you now, didn't I?'

But he ignores me. 'Did you know, for example, how worried I am about my business at the moment, how little work I have, that I'm even having to consider selling my house?'

I shake my head. I think about telling him

that he only has himself to blame, that he should insist on payment for work he's done, but decide it's probably not a very good idea.

'I sympathise with you, Anna, I really do, but it's become so one-sided. Even when we're together, I have the feeling that your mind is somewhere else.'

I get an idea suddenly. 'Is this something to do with you finding Michael with me tonight?'

He doesn't answer right away and I sense things starting to shift my way. He's just jealous and he'll have to admit it and then everything will be okay again.

'It didn't help, no. I realised there's still something going on between you two. I don't mean that you're still in love with him, or he with you. I mean that it just isn't finished yet. And it isn't going to be finished while I'm around.'

I'm really angry now. God, he sounds just like Nell. Of course it's finished with Michael. Again, I think about telling him what happened tonight, how Michael came on to me, how I sussed him, told him what to do with himself. But why should I tell him, why should I have to prove anything?

'So what are you saying? That you don't want to see me any more?' I say this because

I want to scare him, make him see how mad he is making me.

He looks at me for a long time and I begin to feel it turn round again, and now it's me who is scared. He takes hold of my hand and squeezes it. His voice is low when he speaks, almost a whisper.

'I care very much for you, Anna, but yes, that's what I'm saying.'

I pull my hand away from his. I pick up my bag but I can't look at him.

'You'd better take me home, then,' I say, and my voice is remarkably steady.

Morning TV and
Sticky Black Substances

It's six o'clock in the morning and I've been awake all night, looking at my bedroom ceiling, feeling lonelier than I have ever felt before.

But that's okay, because I deserve to be lonely. And I deserve to be lonely because I am a truly horrible person.

Look how horrible I was to my parents, for starters. Those really nice people who took me in when my own mother didn't want me, who looked after me, let me keep my rose bush even though it took up valuable space in the garden, who were so poor they virtually lived on rotten old faggots in gravy. And what do I do in return? I spend my childhood fantasizing about different parents, and then I don't even invite them to my twenty-first birthday party.

No wonder Jack dumped me. No wonder Megan moved so far away. No wonder I found a birth mother from hell. No wonder I married Michael and stayed with him so long.

I deserve no better.

Somehow I manage to get myself out of bed, though I don't feel like doing very much today. But because the dogs need to go out, and because I don't want to be horrible to them, I wrap myself up against threatened rain, and take them for a good long walk before breakfast.

It is a dark, gloomy day, but the rain holds off while I'm walking. There has been quite a lot of rain lately, but the water shortage is still considered serious. How bizarre it all is.

I pick up a paper from the Post Office on the way home, pass the time of day with Helena, just like I always do, as if everything was just great and my life was wonderful, and I realise how easy it is to fool people.

When I get back to the house, I notice that the few remaining leaves on my rose are spotted with black, and I wonder if this is a sign of some kind. A bad sign.

The phone is ringing when I go into the house. It's Nell. She's rung to remind me about tonight. Jack and I are supposed to be going to a party at her house, and I'd forgotten all about it. I tell her I'm not feeling too good, that I don't think I'll be able to make it. She sounds disappointed but it can't be helped. I don't tell her about Jack

276

dumping me. I don't want her coming over and being concerned and nice, and telling me there are plenty more fish in the sea and all that sort of rubbish. I couldn't cope with it.

'By the way,' she says, 'it looks as if Michael's up to no good again. David saw him last night in Leeds, at a club. He was there with some business colleagues, and he spotted Michael with his arm draped around an attractive young blonde.'

He didn't waste much time, I'm thinking. He must have driven into Leeds when he left me, and gone straight on the pick-up. Only I don't say this to Nell.

'Poor Shelly,' I say.

'Are you okay, Anna? You sound a bit down.'

'I'm okay. Just a cold coming on, I think. An early night, and I'll be fine.'

'Nothing I can do, then?'

'Nothing at all.'

I put the phone down and begin to feel restless again, too restless to read my newspaper. So I go into my sitting room, slide into my favourite chair, and just for once, feel sorrier for someone else than I do for myself. I think about ringing Shelly, warning her, but what good would that do? I don't expect she is up to knowing the truth at the moment, and anyway, she'd probably think I was just being vindictive.

I switch on the TV as an escape from my thoughts. There's one of those talk shows on, with an audience telling the presenter all sorts of personal things about their lives. This one's about revenge and what people have done to get their own back on someone who's hurt or upset them, and I'm amazed by some of the confessions. One woman tells the presenter about how she always tenderised meat by stamping on it, before cooking it for her adulterous husband. The audience seem to think this is quite funny, but couldn't it have given him food poisoning? It wouldn't have been very funny then.

Then I stop watching the TV and think about that. About food poisoning, and how bad it can be sometimes. There's been a lot in the news about it lately. People actually dying from it. Then one thing leads to another, and I wonder if it's possible to do it deliberately. Give someone food poisoning, I mean.

And the more I think about it the better it seems. Food poisoning. Not toxic-substance poisoning, which is detectable, but plain old poisoning by everyday food. Why didn't I think of it before? To think of the risk I put myself to when I was feeding strychnine and weedkiller to Michael. I really must have been mad then.

Then it all just sort of falls into place. What I must do, and why I must do it. I must give Michael food poisoning, a deadly dose of it, and I must do it to stop him messing up someone else's life. Someone who probably doesn't deserve to have their life messed up. I must do it for Shelly.

I switch the TV off and get out my trusty encyclopaedia, because if I'm going to do this I want to do it properly. My sense of purpose has returned with a vengeance, and I must look enthusiastic because the dogs are wagging their tails. At least Judd is wagging his tail. Rusty is just watching me, but there is a certain eagerness in his clouded eyes. I think he can read my mind and is egging me on. He never much cared for Michael.

I go into the kitchen again and switch on all the lights, because I hate the gloom, and then I sit down close to my Rayburn. It is very shiny and the lights of the kitchen are reflected all over it. It is glowing as I am glowing.

I turn to 'B' in my encyclopaedia — 'B' for botulism, which off the top of my head is the most deadly form of food poisoning I can think of. I'm right, I find out. It certainly is one of the most deadly forms of food poisoning, and the key phrase, the one which is automatically highlighted for me, is 'often fatal'. It's a pity it's only often fatal, but it will just have to do. Only then I read further and feel even more disappointed. It doesn't tell me how I can come by the *clostridium* bacterium necessary.

But I refuse to be disheartened, so I look around my kitchen for inspiration. There must be plenty of bugs in here. And who knows, with luck, I might just stumble on the right bug. I get up and look in the fridge. This cheers up the dogs whose interest in my plans had fallen off a little. Nothing very useful in here. Ah, but, maybe. I reach into the back of the fridge and find some very out-of-date yoghurt. It should have been consumed on 20 September, which is disgusting, but it happens. Its lid is about to explode which assures me there is no mistake with the date. So I put it on the work surface and get my head back in the fridge. Maybe there is something else in here. There is. A jar of mouldy jam and a half-used tin of tomatoes, also covered in spiky blue mould. I'm doing all right for mould. So what else?

Nothing in the fridge, I fear. Ah, but maybe. Yes, there is something growing in the condensation outlet. I can't quite make out what it is, and it's a bit hard to get at. So I fetch a skewer from my kitchen drawer and dig deep into the hole. I pull out the skewer and it is lined with a sticky black substance that looks as if it might contain every germ known to science. So I get up from my knees and carefully wipe the germ-ridden sticky black substance into the mouldy tomatoes.

Then I open the oven, which I don't use too often, in the hope I left something in there, long, long ago. I haven't unfortunately, well, not real food, but there is a tray of meat fat which must have been there since I last did a roast, which was over a month ago. So out that comes, too.

I go back to my encyclopaedia for more inspiration. I look up *clostridium* separately and am informed that the 'rod-shaped bacterium is widespread in soil', which gives me an excellent idea.

Buzzing now, I go to the freezer and take out some pork fillet that has been sitting in there for ages waiting for me to create something special. I pop it in the microwave and set the control to defrost. It doesn't take long. The dogs are with me all the way again. There is no waning of their interest now. They are wagging their tails and smiling at me.

I remove the long slab of pale-coloured meat from the microwave and take it into the garden. I dig some loose soil away with my hands and cover the meat. The dogs think this is a new fun game of hunt-their-dinner and look all ready to dig it straight up again. So I heave a heavy terracotta pot over on top of the meat, and just to be on the safe side I will keep the dogs out of the garden for a while.

We go back into the house and I ring Michael, at work. He takes my call warily.

I choose my words with care. 'I said some things that I regret last night, and I think we should talk about it. Megan will be home soon and it would be nice if we could be friends, for her sake.' I sound so civilized I'm almost fooling myself. 'How about coming round to dinner tomorrow?'

'I can't make it then,' he says quickly, because I expect he is seeing the attractive young blonde. 'How about Saturday?' he adds coolly, and I can tell that he thinks he has taken the upper hand again, that I am back dangling on the end of his string.

'Saturday's fine.'

* * *

The telephone rings at eight-thirty. I've been awake most of the night thinking, and planning the meal, but I don't feel at all tired.

I feel great, in fact, more alive than I have for ages.

'I've just had a call from Hilary,' Nell says, and she sounds very serious. I can guess what is coming.

'Raymond's told her he's leaving her for another woman.'

'A well-dressed red-head,' I say. 'I saw them together in Leeds when I was Christmas shopping.'

'You didn't say anything.'

'I didn't like to. Is he serious? About leaving, I mean?'

'Deadly. He's already gone. He left last night.'

'But he might come back?'

'Not according to Hilary.'

'How's she taking it?'

'As badly as you'd expect.'

'I'm really sorry,' I hear myself saying, and I mean it, too. 'Are there any decent men left, do you think?'

'Of course there are,' says Nell, because she is married to decent David. 'And anyway, I don't think what Raymond's done makes him bad. I think he's been unhappy for years.'

I don't reply. I'm looking out of my kitchen window, at the upturned terracotta pot.

'Are you okay now, by the way?'

'I feel wonderful.' And I do as well. I've just

had this delightful frisson of pleasure run through me as I think about the pork fillet, which by now, with luck, will be heavily contaminated with *clostridium* bacterium.

Then I remember that I'm not supposed to be feeling wonderful. That I was supposed to be ill yesterday, which is why I missed Nell's party. 'Well, better than I was, anyway. How was the party?'

'It was good, but we missed you. You're sure you're all right? You sound a bit, I'm not sure, but *hyper* is the word which comes to mind. Very different from yesterday.'

'I'm fine, really,' I say, trying not to sound hyper.

'Well, okay, but if you need to talk, whatever, you will call, won't you?'

Just for a moment I'm tempted to tell her everything, then I remember why I am doing what I am doing and think better of it. 'Of course I will.'

She hesitates, then, 'I'm going over to see Hilary this afternoon. I'll keep you posted.'

Sweet and Sour Porc Surprise and Unexpected Weather

What a state I am in this morning. I've just gone through my third night in a row without sleep and I'm so tired and strung up that I can't even bring myself to take the dogs out. I can't be bothered with anything much, not even breakfast. What's the point, when I am going to kill myself?

I made the decision during the night, about three this morning, to be precise. I'd stopped feeling wonderful by then. I was feeling sorry for myself, as usual, thinking how pointless everything seemed, how no one would miss such a horrible person if she wasn't around, then I got this brilliant idea. Why not kill myself at the same time as I'm killing Michael? And once I thought about it, it just made such perfect sense.

The only thing I *can* be bothered with this morning, is the meal I'm going to prepare. I dug up the pork fillet first thing. It's on a plate in front of me now and I could swear I can see rod-shaped bugs squirming about on it.

I've been looking at the meat for ages, and I can stand it no longer. I know it's still early but I've got to do something, so I put my apron on, just like a proper cook, and make a start on my very special dish. I've worked out each step in advance, so I don't even need to consult a recipe book. Which makes me feel a bit like a professional cook, a bit like Delia.

The first thing I do is get the rancid fat from the cooker and flash-fry the meat, just to seal it. I take care not to get it too hot, and kill off any precious rod-shaped bugs. That done, I put the meat to one side, and in the same pan, gently warm up the jam. When that is dissolved, I add the tomatoes and the sticky black substance from the condensation outlet. I find to my pleasure that the blue hairy mould blends surprisingly well with the liquid, and that the sticky black substance provides a useful thickening agent. Then I add a bit of bug-free, none gone-off food, for body, and a few sharper flavourings to balance the sweetness. And finally, to complete my *pièce de résistance*, I add the ancient yogurt.

Then I transfer the meat and the sauce into my very best gold-coloured serving dish and stand back to admire my handiwork. The dogs are wagging their tails, no doubt they are very proud of me.

It doesn't take more than half-an-hour in all. And when it's done, when I've admired it, I sit back and sip coffee and wonder what to call it. I decide on Sweet and Sour *Porc Surprise*, pronounced the French way. This makes me smile. Michael will like that.

The phone rings and I decide not to answer it. I've got the vegetables to think about, and maybe a pudding. I can hear my recorded voice advising the caller to leave a message, then Nell's voice telling me that Hilary has taken an overdose and been rushed to hospital.

Bugger. Trust Hilary to steal my thunder. Except that I'll be successful, of course, whereas I expect she is just playing at it.

I prepare the vegetables and make a straightforward lemon syllabub, which I put in the fridge to chill. Michael likes his syllabub well chilled. Then I tidy up the kitchen so that it's neater and cleaner than it's been for ages.

I think we will eat in here. Nice and cosy. I'll get a candle out. A green one to match the Rayburn. But I don't think I'll lay the table just yet.

I wonder how long it will take to work? The botulism. I don't think it told me that in the encyclopaedia. Ah well, no matter. So long as it does work, I don't really care how long it takes.

★　★　★

The last few hours have been hell. I've never been so restless. I tried watching television but I couldn't sit still. So I made some coffee. Then I had a bath, played soothing music, but I still couldn't relax. So I got out and made more coffee. Then I messed about with my make-up, tried my hair in various new styles, got bored with it all very quickly. Drank coffee. Tried on different outfits, settled for what I put on first thing. Coffee.

At three o'clock, my nerves raw, I nip out to the shop and buy a couple of bottles of indifferent wine. Maybe Michael will bring some but I can't count on that. As I pay for the wine I make it look like I'm in a terrible rush. Luckily, Helena Chopin is chatting to some old dear who's going on about the weather, so I get out of the place without having to be nice or provide explanations as to why I wanted the wine. Helena Chopin is a lovely woman but she can be extremely nosy at times.

It starts to snow while I am walking back. I am amazed. I have been given no warning of this.

When I get back in the house there is another message flashing on my answer-phone. Nell again.

'Just to let you know that Hilary's going to be fine. She's had her stomach pumped, or whatever they do these days, but it looks like she didn't take too many of whatever she took anyway. I just thought you'd like to know. Ring me sometime.'

Typical, I think. What an attention-seeker that Hilary is.

★　★　★

It's late afternoon, and I can't ever remember being quite so edgy before. All that coffee, I expect. I spent ages laying the table, trying different cloths and napkins. I went for plain white linen in the end, even though it's just a bit too formal for the kitchen.

Now I'm looking at the engraving that Michael wanted, that Jack had reframed for me, and I'm wondering why it once seemed so important to hold on to it. How curious I found it. How much I wanted to know what it was all about. Now it just looks like a rather dozy woman and a bunch of stupid cherubs. Not very interesting at all. The only importance it does seem to have, is that it sort of triggered everything off, everything which has led to this day. I should take the dogs out, I know. They're looking forlorn, fed up; they no longer seem very interested in my plans. But I can't take them out because of the snow.

So I ring Harry. I feel that I ought to since I won't be keeping my promise to see him now. And I think I may have been a bit hard on him. I can't possibly put him in the same class as Michael.

'Hello Harry, is it snowing with you?'

'Hello Anna. Yes. Hard. Just like they promised.'

'Who promised?'

'The Met. Office. Haven't you heard? I hope you've got enough dog food to see you over the next couple of days.'

'There's a shop in the village, Harry. Very handy.' Then I realise what he's said. 'What do you mean, a couple of days?'

'There's been a severe weather warning. You haven't heard, have you?'

I think about Michael driving here.

'Does that mean road problems?'

'I'm afraid so. It's lucky it's the weekend; not so much traffic about.'

I look out of the window. The snowflakes are the size of golf balls, and falling so fast the garden has ceased to exist. Why didn't I notice how bad it was getting?

'Are you all right, Anna?'

Suddenly everything seems hopeless. I'd been so looking forward to this evening.

'Anna? Are you still there?'

'Yes.'

'Is everything all right?'

'No. No, it bloody well isn't all right.' And then I'm blubbing and howling and saying all sorts of things I know I shouldn't, but I can't help myself.

★ ★ ★

Nell has arrived with Harry. They are looking at me strangely. They seem worried.

'How did you get here?' I ask them. 'I thought the roads were too bad.'

'Nell picked me up in the Land Rover,' Harry replies. He is looking around him as if he is searching for something in particular.

'Come and sit down, Anna,' Nell is saying. She has her hand on my arm. 'We want to talk to you.'

Might as well, I think. Nothing else to do now. My plans have been completely messed up by the bloody snow. Michael phoned just after I spoke to Harry to tell me he wouldn't be coming.

We sit down in front of the fire. I've built it up high to make me feel cosy. I've left the curtains open so I can see the snow outside. It feels really Christmassy. Especially now, since I brought the holly and mistletoe in, and put sprigs of holly over the pictures and hung mistletoe from the beams. I thought I might as well make a start on decorating the house.

I know why they're here, of course. Me and my big mouth. God knows what I said to Harry.

I've already got rid of the evidence, of course. Safely. I didn't want the dogs getting botulism, if dogs can get it, that is. But you can't be too careful, so I flushed it all down the lavatory.

I've decided not to kill myself after all, not yet, anyway. Because if I die, who's going to kill Michael?

So here we are, all sitting down, all looking into the fire, and I'm waiting for someone to speak. I have decided to play this one by ear.

It's Harry who takes the plunge.

'You said something on the phone, Anna. Something about Michael. Was he coming here for dinner tonight?'

'Yes,' I reply, sounding ever so normal. 'But the snow stopped him.'

'What did you mean about killing him?' This is Nell. I can feel Harry glaring at her.

She wasn't supposed to have just come out with it like that.

I don't know how to answer this. Did I really tell Harry that? I wonder if they'd believe me if I told them it was all a joke. Then I think of the blubbing and howling on the phone to Harry and decide they probably wouldn't.

The dogs are both nuzzling me with their wet noses, though Judd's nose is a lot wetter than Rusty's. I think they feel sorry for me. I think Nell and Harry feel sorry for me, and I hate people feeling sorry for me. I really hate it. It makes me want to cry. It makes me want to cry so much that I do cry. Softly, this time, like the snow falling outside. Big, noiseless tears that go on and on falling.

Cauliflower Soup and Polished Granite Headstones

The snow is melting fast now. I've just looked out of my bedroom window and I can see that I've slept through the best bit. The fun bit. When it's deep, and crisp and even. I can't really remember much about what happened between crying in front of Nell and Harry and the dogs, and waking up with a bloody awful headache a while ago. Just bits.

I remember telling them a little about my thwarted plan.

I remember the doctor coming. (I don't like him much and I think I might have been a bit rude to him.)

I remember some mumbling between the doctor and Nell and Harry, and Nell walking with me up to my bedroom, as if I was an invalid.

Then I'm pretty sure I remember a syringe, and that bloody doctor putting it into my arm.

I remember being force-fed cauliflower soup by Nell.

But not a lot else.

Nell's come into my bedroom and she's looking at me. My room is remarkably tidy, I notice. Gone are the used make-up remover pads and tissues and stuff that I usually dump on the bedside table.

'How long have I been here?'

'A couple of days.'

'It feels more like a couple of weeks.'

'How are you feeling, Anna?'

'I'm not sure,' I tell her. 'A bit weird, drugged up. And I've got a headache.'

She sits on the end of the bed and I notice that she isn't glowing quite as much as usual.

'Why didn't you tell me how bad you were feeling?'

'I didn't feel bad.'

She sighs at this. 'I should have seen for myself.'

I sit up a bit straighter, and my head feels funny. 'Am I drugged up?'

'A little,' Nell says. 'You needed it. The doctor says you've had a bit of a breakdown.'

'A what? Is he mad?'

Nell doesn't answer straight away. 'No, Anna, but I think you were, just a hint.'

So then she tells me how I must have been just a hint mad if I was planning to kill myself and Michael, especially the way I was trying to do it.

'Did you really believe you could conjure up botulism by burying a piece of pork in the garden?'

It does seem pretty preposterous now. Utterly ludicrous, in fact. Then I remember that I'd tried to kill Michael before — twice, in fact, and by much more effective methods. But I decide to keep this to myself.

Entirely to myself. Never to be spoken of to anyone.

★　★　★

I didn't speak of it to the psychiatrist I saw today. I thought she might get me locked up if I did. She seems to think I have been depressed for ages — years, probably — and although I handled the breakup of my marriage well enough, that, and the effects of recent events gradually built up until I just sort of snapped. That makes quite good sense to me, it's just that I *snapped* a bit earlier than she thinks I did — or maybe I didn't so much *snap* before, as *bend* dangerously, and was rescued from snapping-point by Jack. It would have been nice to discuss all this with the psychiatrist, but there was no question of that, of course.

She has prescribed psychotherapy and anti-depressants, and reckons I'll be fine again in a couple of months. It's four days before Christmas now. The day after tomorrow Megan is coming home with Brandon. She doesn't know anything about what's happened lately and I want to keep it that way.

Hilary came round to see me this morning, and she said she knew how I felt. She would happily murder Raymond if she could think of a way of getting away with it. This made me feel a bit better, and for once I actually liked the woman.

I would have asked Nell and Harry not to tell Jack anything, but they must have told him while I was drugged up. They didn't know that he'd dumped me. He came round to the house but I refused, absolutely refused, to speak to him. I can't bear his pity. I don't want him being nice to me just because I've had a bit of a breakdown. I don't want him thinking he's contributed in any way. So I told Nell to send him away and he went.

★ ★ ★

I got up really early this morning. It's the 22nd, and Megan will be home tomorrow, so I have to do it today. Nell has insisted on staying with me till Megan comes, so I've left a note for her to find when she gets up — so that she won't have to worry about me too much.

I get in the car and drive. I drive for a very long time without consulting my map. I don't need to. It's as if I have been pre-programmed. I know exactly where I am going.

I arrive in my old home town mid-morning. I find a call box and ring Nell. Despite my note, I'm worried she might send out a search party or something, so I tell her I'm fine. Really. And that I will be back before dark. I don't tell her where I am, though.

Then I drive to my old house. Only my old house isn't there any more. The prefabs were pulled down years ago to make way for some smarter council houses. It's hard to work out precisely where the old house used to be. Plots have changed and it looks like two houses now take up the space of the prefab, maybe even three.

I park the car and wander up and down, trying to place things. It's drizzling fine rain but I don't let it trouble me. I don't see anyone while I am wandering about. I expect everyone has gone to work or are out Christmas shopping.

A lane runs at the back of the houses, the same lane that ran next to the prefab. So I walk down the lane and when I come to the spot that used to lead into my garden, I find myself thwarted by a high fence. I know it's silly, but I was hoping for a glimpse of my rose bush. It's worse than silly, because it was on its last legs when I left the place. But even though I know it's worse than silly, I still feel vaguely disappointed when I get back into my car.

As I drive through the town centre, I realise that something has changed. Not the town itself, which is still ever so smart with its wide parade, its stuccoed, Regency buildings, and its statue of Queen Victoria outside the town hall. What's changed, is the way I see it. I know that I couldn't live here now, that it's just a bit too smart and neat, and I really have gone off stucco. I prefer natural stone these days.

I drive on, through the shabbier outskirts of the town and head for the cemetery. It is big and impersonal and I wouldn't like to be buried in a place like this. I'd rather be burnt and have my ashes scattered somewhere pretty.

I don't see anyone as I make my way through the big and impersonal cemetery. I know exactly where to go, even though I haven't been here for years. The plot looks uncared for because it is uncared for. The grass has been cut but there are no flowers, as there are on other graves. I thought it was enough to give them an expensive headstone. I was thinking like Michael by the time they died.

I kneel on the grave of my parents, and read the simple inscription which has been tooled out in the polished granite. There's nothing sentimental about it, just the facts. When they were born, and when they died.

Now that I'm here, I'm not at all sure why I came. So I kneel down on the ground and say a few prayers, prayers I haven't said for years but don't seem to have any problem remembering. And it feels quite good. Then I find myself touching the cold, glossy surface of the headstone, and telling them how sorry I am for getting them something like this, something so damn vulgar and flashy, just because it was expensive. Then it all starts pouring out. How sorry I am for thinking about different parents when I was young, for not appreciating them as much as I should have, for not inviting them to that rotten party, and then I shut up and just wait for something to happen. I don't know what. A sign of some kind, perhaps? Some indication of their forgiveness?

I stay there for a long time, waiting for this thing to happen. Until I am shivering and the damp from the ground has soaked into my jeans. Then, when I'm more or less certain that nothing *is* going to happen, when I realise how late it's getting, that if I don't leave soon I won't be home before dark, like I promised — when I start to get up, when I make the sign of the cross, something does happen.

I remember my rose bush again and sink back to my knees.

I remember how I was allowed to keep it, even though it took up so much of my father's precious garden.

And I think that I have my sign.

I wouldn't have been allowed to keep that rose bush if they hadn't loved me so much. And when you love someone as much as that you will forgive them anything.

And then I start to cry again. Not tears of rage, or frustration, or self-pity this time, but tears of genuine sorrow.

Sunsets and Therapy

It's June again and I am better now. The anti-depressants must have helped, I'm sure, but the most valuable part of the treatment was being able to work things out with a clever therapist. Well, the parts I wanted to work out with her, anyway. We talked a lot, of course, but the bit I liked best was the role-play, which involved the use of quite a lot of cushions. I'd never have guessed that psychotherapy could be such good fun.

And I'd never have believed that I'd ever get my head round meditation, either, but I have. I practise for twenty minutes a day now, and I haven't felt this calm in ages. I mean, here I am, ten to ten in the evening, been working flat out since eight this morning, and I'm not a bit tired or stressed.

I've been working so hard to get my shop sorted out. Once I was feeling better, I decided to go back to my plan about starting a business and on Monday morning I open my doors to the public. I am specialising in antiques for dining rooms. This more or less happened by chance; I just found that the things I bid for at auctions were usually suitable for dining rooms. And then, as my acquisitions mounted, I realised that specialisation was probably a very good idea. So that's what I've done, filled the place with beautiful old things for dining rooms: cutlery, candle-sticks, table linen, glassware, you name it. I have laid a single table as a showpiece, and it looks wonderful, though I do say so myself. I can hardly wait to get going now, that's how excited and eager I am. It's a long time since I've been this excited and eager about anything.

Before I close up, I take a last peek at the engraving with the woman and the cherubs. It's not very dining-roomy, I know, but I've marked it at a low price, so with luck it will sell fairly quickly. And the quicker the better. I see it as part of the past now, a part of the past I'd sooner forget.

Despite being so late, because it's June, it's still fairly light as I drive home. And as I drive, I think about what has happened since Christmas — when Megan came home with Brandon and told me that they were married. I wasn't particularly surprised, or upset. It made a lot of sense to me, getting married without fuss and all the problems which come with recently divorced parents. And she was so happy, and Brandon was so thoughtful and caring, that I couldn't not be pleased for them.

It was a good Christmas, an old-fashioned Christmas with lots of silly games and too much to eat and drink. They stayed a week and by the time they returned to sunny California, I felt much stronger. There were a lot of tears, of course, but Megan promised they will visit me at least once a year and I have promised the same. I'm planning my first trip to them in September, and Nell has agreed to look after the shop for me while I'm away.

Raymond went back to Hilary in February but left again a week later. The well-dressed red-head has now entirely disappeared from the scene, but word has it that Raymond is managing very nicely on his own. His divorce from Hilary is imminent and it is expected that she will do very well by way of a settlement. I don't think she'll stay single long. She already has a number of admirers, but the one she seems fondest of is a carpet manufacturer who she thinks bears a striking resemblance to Bill Clinton. I don't see it myself, but there's nothing unusual about that. She's definitely a lot more likeable now, so maybe she was just as unhappy as Raymond clearly was in their marriage, and unhappiness made her a bitch. She's promised to come to my opening on Monday and I'm looking forward to seeing her there.

Michael and Shelly are still together. I haven't spoken to either of them for ages and although Michael is apparently behaving himself a bit more these days, there has, as far as I know, been no more talk of marriage. Either Shelly is getting wiser, or Michael is too fearful of losing yet more of his precious assets in the event of another divorce.

Harry died two months ago. Peacefully, in his sleep. I was very sad, of course, but I know if he could have chosen a way he would have chosen that way. Besides, he went out on a high. His book had just been accepted by a local publisher and he was delighted with all the fuss of it, so delighted in fact, that I heard him laugh out loud for the very first time. We were good friends again by then, I'm glad to say, and nowadays I feel privileged that it was me he chose to talk to about Grace.

There is a glow now on the horizon, a golden, melting glow as the sun finally begins to set. I am nearly home, and the village looks friendlier than it used to look. I am beginning to really enjoy my life here, though I still think about a lemon grove in a place I have not yet discovered. When the shop is paying its way, I might even think about looking for it.

I get out of my car and I see that the lights are on in my house and I can hear the dogs barking. An excited, welcoming bark which makes me smile.

As I put the key in the lock, I notice the scent of my yellow roses. For a while, when I found those black spots on the leaves, I thought it was going to die. But it turned out okay in the end, a bit of something from the garden centre and it's back to its old self now. Better that ever, in fact, because the scent seems stronger than it used to be, or maybe my senses are just sharper now.

I step inside and the dogs pounce on me. Rusty is making a silly noise, his way of showing me how glad he is that I'm home. There is a gorgeous smell coming from the kitchen, and I drop my bag on the floor and follow my nose.

'You look tired,' Jack says, then kisses my cheek.

He has poured a glass of red wine for me and the kitchen table is laid for two. He has even lit a candle.

'Manage to get everything sorted?' he says, ducking to open the oven door.

I tell him I have. Then, while Jack is serving whatever it is that smells so good, I realise how lucky I am to have been given another chance.

All that matters is that I am happy now, and that Jack is happy. It took me ages to see things this way. Weeks of pestering by him to prove that he really did love me, that in dumping me he was just trying to make me see what was happening. Now our relationship is more balanced: I'm not nearly so self-centred as I used to be. I even agreed to meet his parents, which was hard, but I think they liked me. I certainly liked them.

His business has picked up again, thank goodness, and although he is selling his house, it is only because he doesn't need it any more. He lives here with me and the dogs now.

He puts a plate of something gorgeous in front of me and sits down himself. He looks particularly gorgeous tonight and I can hardly wait to get him upstairs.

I know now that I really do love him, and these days for all the right reasons.

I love him so much that if he lets me down I will probably kill him.

We do hope that you have enjoyed reading this large print book.

Did you know that all of our titles are available for purchase?

We publish a wide range of high quality large print books including:
Romances, Mysteries, Classics
General Fiction
Non Fiction and Westerns

Special interest titles available in large print are:
The Little Oxford Dictionary
Music Book
Song Book
Hymn Book
Service Book

Also available from us courtesy of Oxford University Press:
Young Readers' Dictionary
(large print edition)
Young Readers' Thesaurus
(large print edition)

For further information or a free brochure, please contact us at:
Ulverscroft Large Print Books Ltd.,
The Green, Bradgate Road, Anstey,
Leicester, LE7 7FU, England.
Tel: (00 44) **0116 236 4325**
Fax: (00 44) **0116 234 0205**

Other titles in the
Ulverscroft Large Print Series:

STRANGER IN THE PLACE

Anne Doughty

Elizabeth Stewart, a Belfast student and only daughter of hardline Protestant parents, sets out on a study visit to the remote west coast of Ireland. Delighted as she is by the beauty of her new surroundings and the small community which welcomes her, she soon discovers she has more to learn than the details of the old country way of life. She comes to reappraise so much that is slighted and dismissed by her family — not least in regard to herself. But it is her relationship with a much older, Catholic man, Patrick Delargy, which compels her to decide what kind of life she really wants.

NOVEMBER TREE

Ann Stevens

Rowena and Phyllida are both sixty-something, and both on their own — so what better than sharing their declining years? They have known each other for fifty years — and there's something to be said for the devil you know. But who said that retirement would be peaceful? Amidst demanding relatives and with a new suitor on the horizon, it looks as though the future is far from predictable, bringing past resentments and a festering secret to the surface. As the tension rises and tolerance falters, the long-suppressed truth threatens to erupt in a most unpredictable way.

COME HOME TO DANGER

Estelle Thompson

Charles Waring has come home to Queensland to attend his mother's funeral and his remark, intended only for a family friend to hear, is inadvertently overheard by several other people. The chain of events which follows convinces Charles that his mother was murdered because she knew a terrible secret from someone's past, and he finds himself in a deadly game of cat-and-mouse as he tries to unravel the mystery. Meanwhile, he must face the certainty that someone among those he has come to care about poses a cruel threat.

SUMMER OF SECRETS

Grace Thompson

When Bettrys Hopkyns' alcoholic sister Eirlys committed suicide, Bettrys was determined that Eirlys's baby daughter Cheryl — the result of Eirlys's secretive summer love affair — would stay with her. Still yearning for Brett, her former lover, Bettrys sets herself a challenge: to find Cheryl's father. Her search takes her and Cheryl to a small seaside village in west Wales; to a close-knit community seething with secrets. Befriended by the cheerful Gordon, who falls in love with her, Bettrys is quickly drawn into a web of deceit and is forced to face the terrifying possibility that Brett might be a murderer . . .